A BROTHER'S SALVATION

SACRED HEARTS MC
BOOK 14

A.J. DOWNEY

COPYRIGHT

≈

Edited by Barbara J. Bailey

Book design by Maggie Kern

Cover art by Dar Albert at Wicked Smart Designs

DEDICATION

To Carrie, Barbara, Martha and Mary. My personal cheer squad to get me through this book. It wouldn't be half of what it is without you.

1

D ragon…

I sighed and stretched out along the new spring grass, laying on my back under a wide blue sky, the odd fluffy fat white cloud skating across the pure blue surface. The sun was out, the weather warm, but it wasn't hot. It was still too early for that. Hell, we were lucky it wasn't fuckin' snowing. We'd had some late winters in recent years, so having an actual spring was a real nice change of pace. I breathed in slow, deep, and even, and cleared my throat.

"Hey baby, I missed you. Wanted to get here sooner, but I'm definitely getting older and the cold just ain't agreeing with me much anymore."

I smoothed a hand over the tickling fresh green and fought the urge to light up a smoke. She hated that I smoked and so I didn't do it here, when I was with her like this.

I let my hand rest on the ground, the sun warming me through my leathers, and closed my eyes. If I imagined it hard enough, I could almost feel her hand, under the grass, under all that fuckin' dirt my misdeeds put her under. If I breathed real slowly, I could almost hear her laugh, hear her talking to me; and even though she was gone, I still lived for those moments. Even all these years later.

"God, I miss you, Tilly," I murmured. I sniffed, and let out a breath. I wouldn't cry about it, but sometimes, even now, even years later, it was a near thing.

I rooted in the inside jacket pocket of my coat and pulled out the rumpled picture I'd brought with me.

"Our boy done good, baby. Just look at that little man." I held up the picture above us, over to the side so that she could see.

"One year old and counting. Strong, just like his Pop-Pop, and strong-willed, just like you. You should see our son with him, baby. He makes such a good dad. Way better 'n me. Raisin' Dray, that was all you, sweetheart. I damn sure can't take credit. That was *all* you."

I closed my eyes and stared at the fire on the insides of my eyelids, listening, straining to hear her laugh, her voice, like I sometimes did and instead felt my heart plummet when I heard weeping instead. I was drawing a deep breath to console her when I realized that it didn't have the same quality as when I heard her the other times. When I heard my Tilly, it came from both nowhere and everywhere at the same time. This weeping, this broken-hearted crying came from behind us... where my brothers were buried.

I frowned, and the light spring breeze carried with it the faint scent of roses and the sound of weeping with it. I smoothed a hand over the grass covering my wife and sighed.

"Sorry, baby. I'll come back, I promise."

I pushed up off the ground and stood, my body creaking a little more than it used to, and peered through the wrought-iron bars surrounding the section of cemetery holding my brothers' plots. I couldn't see anything around the backs of the standing grave markers, but the heavy, broken sobbing was definitely coming from that direction. I worried for a minute that it was Hayley, but the voice wasn't quite right; it was unfamiliar to me.

I took a halting step forward, past my wife and towards that back fence and paused. I didn't want to scare the shit out of anybody, but I didn't have a name to call out. I scraped my bottom lip between my teeth and settled for a "Hey, yeah, who's there?"

The sound suddenly ceased, and I caught a flash of copper as a woman stood. I scowled, not because I was pissed or anything that she was there, but on account of the fact I had no clue who she was.

I took a step forward and she took a step back.

"Hey, wait!" I called, but she had turned, mute, and fled. I made strides but there weren't no back gate to the group of plots, so I had to make my way around. By the time I reached even with the front of the wrought-iron fence, she was ducking into her car.

"I just want to talk to you!" I called, but she started up and took off. I squinted and managed to get a good portion of her plate, but not all of it. Still, with the make, model, and color of the car, it should be enough. I pulled out a worn out notepad from my cut, and a pen, jotting the information down.

I turned, the slight easy wind that rustled the trees sweeping the mild drama away, the cemetery returning to its peaceful silence. I scanned the stones in front of me and picked out the one that she'd popped up from behind. I let myself in the little gate and went to it, squinting at the print. Damn eyes were gettin' bad. Was lucky I was able to get the numbers and letters off of her plate at the distance that I did. I pulled out my reading glasses and put them on.

"The fuck?" I said aloud, though I kept my tone muted outta respect.

Still, outta all the brothers a broad could get worked up over, Dura-cell was the *last* one I expected. Don't get me wrong. Once a brother, always a brother. You fight for 'em, you die for 'em, and they do the same for you or-fucking-else, but Cell? Cell was a different animal from the rest of us. Charming, cunning, but a cold piece of work and a fucking liability. If he'd tried to patch in to my chapter, it never woulda happened, but he hadn't come from my chapter. He'd come from up yonder and he had brought Blue with him.

Blue was a good man, and what was done was fucking done. I hadn't had a good enough reason to pull Cell's patch, and to lose Cell would have meant losing Blue and I hadn't wanted that to happen to poor Blue. It'd been a blessin' in disguise that Cell'd bit it like he did, though you'd probably never hear me admit that shit out loud.

"Well, ain't you a mystery?" I muttered, thinking back to the woman. She'd been older than Cell by, like, a lot, but younger than me. Probably late forties, early fifties, if I had to guess. Her hair, while copper, had that color of deeper copper that said good salon dye rather than natural, and didn't have the stiff quality of most natural gingers' locks. It'd tousled with the wind and had lost, ruffling in the breeze and sparking fire from the glint of the sun on it.

She'd been willowy and light on her feet, dressed like most conservative white women around these parts, in jeans that'd looked like they'd seen an iron and a simple western blouse. She had brown and worn-in cowgirl boots on her feet as she'd dashed across the sweeping drive through the cemetery to her car, a modern Honda CRV.

I stood for a long time staring at the marble gravestone of our most-recently-fallen brother and gave a grunt. I had a feeling I knew who it could have been, but I didn't want to jump to any conclusions. I let out a gusty sigh and stared over the stones of my brothers, through the wrought-iron fence at the back of the white marble stone that was my wife's.

I hated that our visit had been cut short, but another, stiffer breeze carried with it a breath of rose scent and I knew she was tellin' me to go. She knew I loved a good mystery, and this one needed solvin' before I could let it go completely.

4

"See you around, boys," I muttered and went back around, stopping at Tilly's plot to leave behind the photo of our grandson.

"Be back soon, baby. Promise."

I went down the back side of the carefully-manicured green hill to my bike, which the terrain had hidden from her, just as her car had been hidden from me. I stepped off the yellow curb and rang up my man, Data.

"What up, D?"

"Need you to break into the DMV for me; got a partial plate, make, model, and color."

"Gimme what you got."

I told him, reading off my notepad, and listened to him clack away on his keyboard through the line.

"Got it," he confirmed. "When you want it by?"

"See if you can beat me, I'm on my way in now."

"You're on; loser pours the drinks."

I grinned and chuckled. "Fair enough."

I hung up without bothering to say good-bye and got onto the front of my bike. I took my time putting on my helmet and pulling on some gloves. The weather was warm, the sun beating down, sure, but once you got going, the wind still had a bite and some chill to it. Spring had barely sprung and it was a little late doing it this year. A good part of the country still had snow, but for some reason, this pocket of Kentucky was a sunny, lush green paradise.

I enjoyed the waveing bluegrass as I rode out towards the club, and went through a couple of the outlying farms in the area to get there. I went the long way, though even if I'd cut through town, Data would probably still have beat me to it. I wanted him to. Some things in life were just more important than winning all the damn time. I'd learnt that lesson the hard way and I tried like the devil to avoid making the same mistakes twice, let alone over the little things.

I pulled up in front of the club and backed my bike in; Data waited at the door, a sheaf of printouts in one hand, arms crossed over his chest.

"What are yah havin'?" I called out, and he grinned.

"Whatever you're pourin', P."

I chuckled and walked across the gravel, thumping Data on the back as he turned to walk into the barroom with me. He took a seat up on one of the stools at the bar while I lifted the leaf and walked on through to play bartender. I raised my eyebrows at him as he noisily squared the edges of the pages against the scarred bar top. I grinned and figured he was enjoying this a little too much, but what the hell.

"So, what're you havin'?" I asked, playing the part.

"I think this calls for your finest Kentucky bourbon, P."

"Oh yeah?"

"Ah, yeah. I got just about everything you could want and then some."

Color me intrigued. I pulled down the top-shelf bourbon from a local distillery we liked and brought two glasses out from under the bar. Data held up the first sheet of paper and said, "Your mystery woman's name is Martha Lanham, but she goes by Marcie, according to all her social media posts."

"Ah-huh." I slid two fingers of bourbon his direction and without taking his eyes off the page he picked up the glass, breathed deep the aroma, and sipped.

"Mm, she lives at 1403 West Hazelton Avenue in town there, works at the Super Clips as a hairdresser, the one on 152nd, has two daughters, an ex-husband… and the coup de grace?"

He eyed me above the third sheet of paper, two lying discarded face-down on the bartop after he'd read off their information. I took a sip out of my own bourbon glass and swallowed, the bite of the alcohol mellowing out into a smooth burn.

"Don't leave me hangin' right before the big finish, boy," I grumbled.

"There's a police report filed with her name on it with county. An accident report. Motor vehicle collision with a single rider out on the old highway and Evan's Lake Road."

"Which explains why she was all busted up at Duracell's grave."

Data shook his head and a look like sympathy crossed his face. he took another sip of bourbon and sighed, heavy, and I told him, "Speak your mind, brother."

"Cell was one of us, P. By the time he came to us he was already locked and loaded and a member of the club, but if he'd been given another year, I don't think that'd be the case. He was one of us in name only, and I feel guilty to a degree saying it out loud, but we were all thinking it."

"Cell was a pain in the ass," I agreed "But he *was* our brother when he died."

Data nodded and huffed out a breath and I knew what he was thinkin'. Hell, I was thinkin' the same thing. Out of anyone and everyone that woman should feel absolutely no guilt over killin', Cell was certainly it. Who knew how many untold deaths she may have avenged? Who knows how many more lives she saved?

Data was right. Cell had been headed down a path and none of us were sure we'd be able to rein him in. He was destined for a quick death in a blaze of glory or a lifetime behind bars, and I wasn't right sure how many of us he meant to take down with him if it suited him. Cell didn't give a good goddamn about anyone but himself. Certainly not Blue, and definitely not Hayley. He was a born sociopath and we all knew it.

Marcie Lanham had done the world a kindness that day, there just weren't no telling *her* that. Of course, that was supposin' someone had tried. Bein' that she was a citizen, I had no doubts someone had. The townsfolk had no idea the horrors we'd kept from knockin' on their doors, they just saw us as the boogey man. They weren't wrong, but there was a lot worse than us out there, that was for damn sure.

"What cha thinkin', P?" Data asked me.

"Don't rightly know just yet," I told him honestly.

"Oh, come on, something is going on up there," he said with a wink.

I gathered up the sheets of paper with all her info on them and stacked them, creasing them once down the middle and tucking the pile into the inside pocket of my jacket.

"Shut up and drink your bourbon," I told him. with a grin to take any of the bite out of the order. He grinned back and nodded, taking another sip.

"Don't even think about it," Doc declared without even looking up from the tattered paperback. I dropped into the lounge chair next to his and sighed.

"You don't even know what I'm about to ask," I said.

"Oh, yes, I do, and it ain't happening. This one is all you, Compadre."

"Shit," I muttered with a sigh.

Doc looked over his half-moon specs at me and harrumphed, shaking his head.

"You *were* gonna ask me, weren't you?"

"Yeah, I figured it was worth a shot."

He shook his head like he was disappointed I would even think it and I kind of had to admit, he had me there.

"Chandra was the love of my life, same as Tilly was yers, asshole."

"I know it," I groused and slid down in the outdoor lounger, resting my chin on my chest and my hands, fingers laced, across my stomach.

"I knew you was gonna hit me up as soon as Data told me about it," he said with a sigh and I raised an eyebrow in his direction.

"Yeah? How's that?"

"Because you're a conniving bastard and for some reason, when that conniving ain't towards something illegal, you've managed to turn your happy ass into some kind of match-making babushka."

I laughed and it came out a smoker's laugh, rumbling in my chest and heavy with phlegm. I hocked some up and spat to the side, and just to give the finger to the gods that fuckin' kept me here, I pulled out a cig, tapping the filter against the side of my pack before sticking it between my lips.

"Because that'll make it better," Doc muttered.

"Shut it," I grumbled.

"I'm a doctor," he reminded me, and I rolled my eyes. That was pretty much the end of *that* conversation and we returned to the original topic at hand.

"I ain't lookin' to hook up," I told him and he sighed.

"Then don't hook up," he said with a shrug. "But don't expect me to handle this one for you. God love you, you're on your fuckin' own this time. You found her, and finders' keepers, motherfucker."

I scowled. "I just told you, I ain't lookin' to hook up."

"So you ain't," he agreed. "I'm lookin' for less than even that. Now leave this old man alone with his memories," he said softly, and the hurt was apparent enough in his tone that all I could do was heave a heavy sigh.

"Never wanted you, of all people, to know what that felt like," I muttered and he gave a stiff nod.

"I know, and I know it ain't your fault, or the club's fault, or any of that shit. We didn't go lookin' for trouble…"

"Yeah, but trouble found us anyway." I heaved a sigh. "I miss her, too, Doc."

"We all do," he agreed with a battered sigh.

A long silence ensued, comfortable despite how broken we both were. I sighed finally, one sorry son of a bitch. Sorry didn't fix nothin' though. Didn't serve a purpose. Only action fixed this kind of hurt; my deal was, I didn't want it to be fixed.

"I tell you somethin' without you thinkin' I've gone crazy?" I asked.

He lowered Chandra's battered old paperback to his knee and balanced it on the fraying denim there.

"What's up?" he asked, scowling, about as serious as I felt.

"You heard how I came upon this one, right?"

"Data said she was at the cemetery, caterwaulin' over Cell's grave." I gave a short nod. "I assume you were there for Tilly," he added softly and I nodded again.

"It's been a while," I said, "but sometimes, I catch the smell of roses, you know? Other times it's like I can almost hear her."

"And this morning?" he asked.

"Both, and I do mean it's been a long time since I've had either."

"What, you think Tilly was tellin' you something?" he asked.

I nodded, "Still had to see if you might be interested in putting this one to rights."

Doc shook his head, "All you, José."

I reared back and looked at him hard. "Been a lot of years since you called me by my given name."

He sniffed and gave a shrug. "Seemed like the situation called for it."

I nodded and got up, rotating my shoulders to loosen them up a bit.

"Where you goin'?" he asked with mild interest.

"Guess I'm goin' to get a haircut," I said, and he snorted a laugh like he couldn't quite believe me.

"You're serious," he said incredulously.

I nodded. "Only sure thing in life is that it's always changing," I said with a heavy sigh.

"Really? I thought sure it was something about death and taxes."

I laughed, coming up short.

"That too."

2

M arcie...

I froze. Which was funny, because he froze too, just inside my little one-woman-show of a salon door. Except, where adrenaline and a little fear coursed through me, he had a cock-sure attitude painted on his face; one eyebrow slightly raised, lips curved in an amused smile. I couldn't tell if he was trying to be intimidating or not, but he was.

Well, when it came to the attitude, two could play at that game and I did. Raising an eyebrow of my own and standing a little straighter, I asked in my sweetest retail voice, "Can I help you?"

"Lookin' fer a haircut if yer available," he said.

Right.

"I'm available," I said, my curiosity winning out. He ducked his head in a nod and came around the counter back to my work area. He took off his coat with the faded and dirty patches all over it, the smell of burnt tobacco wafting over. I wrinkled my nose at the offending smell of old cigarettes and was glad it was behind his back. I still wasn't sure why exactly he was here and it felt awfully like I'd invited a venomous snake into my home – even though I didn't live here.

Still, I had to figure if he knew where I worked that quickly, he knew where I lived. It wasn't exactly a stretch. I watched him hang his coat on the hook by the mirror of my station and met his dark eyes in that mirror. He stepped over and settled into my chair.

I licked dry lips and said, "I'm going to tuck your collar, if you don't mind."

"I ain't here to make your job harder, you just do what you do, Sweetheart."

Okay...

"Why exactly *are* you here?" I asked, rolling the collar of his black-and-red checkered flannel shirt under. I made sure it was tucked securely over the back of the faded black tee shirt he had on underneath it and pulled a fresh drape off the neat stack of them I had on a shelf between my station and the next. My salon had three chairs to it, but I worked alone. I didn't need another stylist to make my bills or the rent on this old place, but I still had a "Help Wanted" sign in the window anyways. It wasn't a struggle, but it was still a bit tighter financially around here than I liked, some months.

"I told you, lookin' fer a haircut," he said and I braced my fists on my hips and arched a brow at him over his head. He chuckled and settled in.

"Now, I know you aren't trying to bullshit me none," I told him, my Kentucky accent thickening.

"Nope," he said, grinning.

"Good, 'cause y' can't. I've raised two daughters as ornery as me and y' can't bullshit a bullshitter. I've seen and done it all."

He laughed at me and waved me down with a hand saying, "Wouldn't dream of tryin' to get one over on you, Mrs. Lanham. Wouldn't dream of it."

"It's '*Ms.*', thank you very much. I ain't been 'Mrs.' anything going on three years now. Ever since I caught my girl's daddy cheating."

"Good to know," he said gently.

"So what's your name?"

"They call me Dragon," he stated, carefully looking me up and down in the mirror in front of us.

"Folks call me Marcie," I said. "You can, too. Now, what d'you think you want to do here?"

"Your guess is as good as mine, Marcie," he said and let out a gusty sigh. "Kept my hair long like this since I was a teenager."

"Uh-huh." I sounded doubtful because I was. "Are you sure you want a drastic change?" I asked.

His eyes met mine and the weight, the seriousness in them, struck me to my core. He said to me, "Life is full of changes, Darlin'. It's most definitely time for a change in mine." I felt my mouth go a little dry and nodded carefully.

"Well," I said calmly, even though my pulse raced. "This particular change won't take much at all. What do you normally do for your hair?"

It was a little bit of business as usual after that while we settled on what to do for him. He was a no-fuss-no-muss kind of a man, as was evidenced by the state of his hair. It was healthy for the most part, but he used a harsh shampoo and forget about conditioner. Who knew how long it had been since it had last been cut. I mean, he was a handsome man, but I was sure he would be much more... Well. I didn't need to be thinking along those lines, now did I? Not when I'd first encountered him only this morning in the cemetery.

"So, you mind telling me what you were doing this morning?" he asked, breaking the ice, so to speak.

"Nothing I'd right like to talk about," I said, and finished combing out his long hair, putting it back into a loose ponytail.

"Well, then, what would you like to talk about, Marcie? Seems to me I'm going to be here a while."

"How about what were *you* doing there this morning?"

"Visiting my wife," he said succinctly. I gave one long, slow blink, both taken aback and in a bid to buy myself some time to properly react. I mean, I didn't know how to react.

"I'm sorry," I said, automatically, and scraping my bottom lip between my teeth asked, "You sure you're ready for this?"

"No," he said softly, shaking his head slightly, his gaze locked on my face in the mirror. I got the impression he wasn't talking about his hair and the look he gave me was so intense, so full of a silent disquiet, I had to suppress a shudder.

"No?" I echoed.

"No, so now's as good a time as any to do it. Go on now, pull that trigger," he said.

I squeezed the handles of my shears together and cut crisply through all that thick hair. He grinned at me and said softly, "Attagirl."

"I'm not a horse or a dog," I said tersely, but with a smile on my lips.

He flashed a grin at me through his salt-and-pepper beard and I shook my head chuckling softly, wondering why in the world I was feeling so giddy all of a sudden, trying to remember how long it had been, when I'd last felt anything like it.

"Better behave or I'll shave you right down the middle," I teased as I ran my fingers through his thick hair and shook it out. That garnered a laugh.

"I believe you'd do it, too. I promise, I'll be a good boy." He winked at me and I felt myself blush furiously. I couldn't remember the last time *that* had happened either.

"Why don't you come on over to the bowl," I said. "Get you washed up so I can give you a proper cut."

He stood up and stretched, and wandered over with a slow and easy roll to his gait. I set a towel down to cushion his neck from the hard porcelain rim of the sink and had him sit and lean all the way back.

There was a certain kind of intimacy when you washed another person's hair for them. But in a salon setting, there was also a sort of an impersonal business-like divide between stylist and customer. With our light and teasing banter just a moment before, even though my hands went through the motions and did the job at hand, starting the water, checking the temperature, this felt different. Probably it was because I was so far left of center from where I usually was. It wasn't just over the heartache and grief I still carried over killing his man, but also because of the way he looked up at me now. Eyes were dark and glittering with calculation, slightly hooded as I worked above him.

I wet his hair and asked if the temperature was all right. He gave a slight nod and murmured, "It's good," and I was relieved when he closed his eyes, and his expression became almost meditative, like so many people when they had their hair washed. I was sure I was no different when I had my hair done.

Who knows, I thought dryly, *if I do a good job, he might not kill me.*

My thoughts drifted to a fantasy movie I had watched with my two girls all while they were growing up and the line: *"Good night, Westley. Good work. Sleep well. I'll most likely kill you in the morning."* Except while it was a cute and kitschy line in a movie, the man whose hair I shampooed right now most likely could and would kill me for what I'd done a year ago.

I'd gone to make my turn and had run smack into one of his club members on his motorcycle. He'd lain broken and bleeding on the pavement, had looked into my eyes and his final words would forever haunt me…

"Should have looked twice. I had people to go home to."

"Marcie?"

I took in a sharp breath and came back to myself. Inquisitive dark eyes, glittering cold and calculating, looked up at me and I shook my head.

"Sorry," I said. "Got a bit lost for a moment."

"You done getting that shit out of my hair?" he asked.

"What? Oh, yeah."

"Good." He sat up and I sprung to action, turning off the sink and scrambling for a towel.

"Stop," he said, and though he wasn't loud, his voice was firm.

I stilled instantly, and frowned at that. I wasn't used to letting anybody boss me around, usually *I* was the bossy one.

"It's just a little water, and water never hurt nothin'. Now, let's stop with the bullshittin' and get down to business. Why were you at the cemetery this morning?"

I licked my suddenly-dry lips and answered him truthfully, "Guilt, fear, heartache – take your pick, Mr. Dragon."

He searched my face and said, "Most citizens wouldn't feel that over killin' the likes of one o' us."

I recoiled in horror at first, but I could see his point. He wasn't talking about me necessarily, though I was definitely 'other' as compared to whatever world they lived in because their world was most definitely not the same as ours. From what I knew, their world was a place of violence and blood. The stories of shootouts, madness, and mayhem painted the evening news in flashes of blue and red as policemen milled about shaking their heads over yellow-draped piles that used to be men.

He stood in front of me, his hair dripping; streams of water slipped down the black hairdresser's drape and his expression was softened with something akin to pity. I swallowed hard and he said, "Ain't nothin' bad gonna happen to you, Marcie. You got my word on that. I'm just curious is all."

"Curious about why I was in the cemetery," I said, and he nodded.

"That's right."

"Well, now you know," I said, pursing my lips.

God, I felt like I was having another full on melt-down like I had that morning. It was too much. One minute I was doing all right and the next I was swinging the opposite way. You'd think a woman in her fifties would have her shit together.

He searched my face, his expression failing at 'neutral', curiosity apparent as he tried to decide one way or the other about me. Finally, he asked me, "You want I should go?"

I blinked in surprise, and said, "Well, not like that, you don't! Sit down and let me finish your hair. I honestly don't know what's wrong with me lately. I don't know what my problem is. I sure don't plan on charging you for being subjected to this hot mess." I fussed over him and finally got a bit bossy when he wouldn't budge. "Will you *sit down*?"

He cracked a crooked grin at that, and with a single nod, went back to my cutting chair and sat down. I toweled off the worst of the wet and got myself together enough to focus on giving him a decent cut. I wouldn't, I *couldn't,* send him out of my shop looking half-assed. That wasn't what I was about and it never would be.

"My son-in-law was in a bad accident last night," I said, finally. "My girl, Devon, called me up out of the blue at two this morning to tell me he was going into surgery."

"I'm sorry to hear that," he said, and he sounded it.

"I don't know," I murmured, heaving a heavy sigh. "Maybe it's Karma."

"Don't believe in it," he said with a shrug.

"Y'don't?"

"Well," he hedged, "maybe I do, but not for people like you. Just for men like me."

"People like me?" I put my hands on my hips and demanded, "Now, just what is *that* supposed to mean?"

He chuckled and shook his head. I arched an eyebrow and had some second thoughts on sending him out onto the street with his hair half-done lookin' like a jackass.

"Means it doesn't happen to people like you, you know, *nice* and what society considers normal."

"Pretty sure society doesn't have much to do with Karma, don't you think? It's what you done put out into the world, coming back at you."

"Then wouldn't that mean your son-in-law done put something out into the world Karma disagreed with?"

I'd resumed cutting his hair but hesitated, thinking about what he'd said.

"I suppose that makes sense," I murmured, finally.

"You don't mind me askin', what makes you think you didn't do the world a favor and that Cell's Karma wasn't comin' back to pay a visit through you that day?"

"That's a horrible thought!" I cried and he met my eyes in the mirror; his were cold, hard, and glittering with intelligence that was downright frightening. I swallowed hard and blinked and asked, "What would even make you say something like that about your own man?"

"I knew him; you didn't. And you didn't answer my question."

"I- I don't know," I stammered, at a loss for words.

I closed my mouth, and focused on cutting, letting the conversation die for the time being. I was surprised to find that the silence we lapsed into wasn't at all an uncomfortable one. I hadn't expected that.

To be honest, given what I knew about the club from the evening news and the swathe of mayhem and destruction they'd dragged through this town back in the day, him coming here like this, quiet and working very hard at *not* being intimidating? Well, he wasn't at all what I expected from one of the likes of him.

That turned the rest of my day into one full of deep thoughts and intro-spection.

3

D ragon...

"Woah-ho-ho! What the fuck is this shit?" Reaver crowed as I walked through the front door of the club later that night.

"I'll be damned," Trigger echoed in disbelief.

"That's *so* not right," my son said over both their heads. He was standing by the table both Trig and Reave were sittin' at, and had his boy flopped against his shoulder. Little man was out like a fuckin' traffic light, drooling on his daddy's cut. I smiled at the sight and remembered when it was Dray droolin' against mine when he was a wee tyke.

"Figured it was time for a change," I said. "Don't it make me look more distinguished?"

"Makes you look like a fuckin' citizen," my boy groused and I chuckled.

"Goddamnit, Dray! What did we talk about when it came to language in front of Stephen?" Evy walked out from behind the bar and smiled at me. "It looks good, Papa D," she said affectionately, using my name we used for the kid. I honestly didn't feel like a 'grandpa', but feel like one or not, I was one. Honestly never thought I'd live to see the day, always figured it'd be Tilly here and me long gone. Not the other way around.

The pang of lonesome misery was sharp and immediate, but as each year went by, dulled off quicker and quicker. I didn't know what to make of that, honestly; wasn't sure I liked it. Just like I wasn't sure about Dray and Everett naming their boy after her daddy, who was long gone... but, I had to admit, the name was growing on me quicker than the pain was fading. I was just glad they hadn't named him after me.

"What you scowling at, boy?" I grumbled.

"Only time I ever seen your hair this short was when you came home from prison when I was thirteen," he said flatly.

I chuckled and shook my head, only reason it'd ended up short that time was the lice infestation at the state pen. I'd gone up on a nickel but had been out in two. It'd taken three years to get it out back long again.

"Yeah, well, seemed like the right thing to do."

"Uh-huh, right," Trig said dubiously.

"You're next, big man."

"Over my dead-ass fuckin' body," he grumbled and raised an eyebrow at Reave, who just sat there grinnin' like a loon.

"I think it's safe to hand him back, now, babe," Everett murmured and Dray handed their son back to her.

"Won't go down for y', huh?" I asked.

She rolled her eyes and forced a smile over her gritted teeth.

"Only for his daddy," she said.

"It's a phase. That one," I jabbed a finger at Dray, "did the same damn thing when he was Stevie's age."

"Stephen," Everett automatically corrected. She had a thing, like her dad, she said, about shortening a perfectly good name. I smiled and she leaned over and kissed Dray.

"Be in in a little while," he said gently.

"Better be," she murmured huskily. My boy smiled and didn't even hide the fact he was checking his woman out.

She grinned, a feral look and I asked, "When the fuck you two gettin' hitched, again?"

"Language," she reminded sharply, even though the baby was out. "And, whenever he decides to put a ring on it," she shot over her shoulder as she stalked away, light on her feet in that graceful dancer's way that she had.

I raised an eyebrow at my son and he raised both of them back at me. I nodded and said, "Grab the tequila and let's talk."

"Meet you out back," he said, adding, "none of the rest of you fuckers are invited."

"Fuck you, too," Trig said, laughing.

My boy grinned, "Pretty sure I just fucked you first, asshole."

Reave laughed like a maniac and Trigger's booming laugh rolled out across the common room. It felt like we'd missed an opportunity when it came to a road name, just then. Shoulda named him Thor.

I went out back, shakin' my head and chuckling, expecting to run into more of the guys, but it was quiet. Dani had the big bay doors open on her shop, and gave me a nod as she went to and fro, between her little forge and work table. Red ducked around the corner of the door and gave a wave and went back to sitting near his woman, the two talking, Dani smiling at whatever he had said.

Those two were a pair. I was proud of how far both had come. Best friends always did tend to make the best lovers. That's what my Tilly had been for me. My best friend, my woman, my confidant. Mother of my child; my everything…

Until you killed her.

That voice of self-loathing and derision was always present whenever I thought of her anymore, and I hated it, but bore that cross just the same because it was true. It may not have been my hand that pulled the trigger, but the blood was all over my hands just the same. It was my choices, my decisions, that'd written my woman's name on that bullet. It was me.

I walked up to the big fire-pit and gave a nod. The fire had been set by someone for tonight and I aimed to take advantage. I walked over and pulled out my trusty Zippo, the one Tilly had bought for me, with the roses on it and the back engraved. I flicked back the lid with that satisfying click and rolled my thumb over the wheel, lighting her up. I touched the flame to the paper of the presto log under the wood and got it going before snapping the lid closed and putting it back in my pocket.

I crouched there, watching the flames lick along the paper and char the wood and felt my old emotional wounds throb, burn, and ache – though admittedly, not as keenly as they once did. The first indication that my boy was coming up on me was the scuff of his boot against the gravel behind me.

"Spill it, Old Man. What's eating at you?" he asked.

I stood up, my knees popping, a groan escaping my mouth even as my joints groaned in unison to the sound. I was starting to feel every bit of my age lately, and I blamed it squarely on being a grandpa.

"Went and saw your mom this morning," I said with a sigh, looking my son over.

Immediately, his expression became guarded, shuttered. I knew we didn't talk about her nearly as often as we should; I also knew it was something he wanted, but I hated doing it because of the look on his face right now. Which I knew he didn't even know he did.

"Yeah?" he asked, and his voice was guarded against his own hurts.

He gestured over to two of the solid wood loungers in front of the fire with the tequila bottle and I went to one while he came around and dropped into the other. He set the bottle and two glasses down on the little table between them and I picked it up, uncorking it and pouring a couple of fingers into each glass.

"Yeah," I echoed. "Was a good visit. Showing off that boy of yours. Your mama would be damn proud of you, boy. I know I am."

"Yeah?" he repeated, the flavor of the word taking on the seasoning of surprise.

"Hell, yeah," I said gruffly, and handed him one of the glasses. "Just wish you'd put a fuckin' ring on that girl's finger. Make it permanent."

"About that..." he drawled carefully.

"You want the ring I gave your mama?" I asked.

"Would you be cool with that?"

"Anyone else, I'd probably say go pick something out at the jewelers, or have Dani make you something, but for her?" I reached into the inside pocket of my jacket and pulled out the worn red velvet ring box I kept Tilly's set in, close to my heart. I handed it over and was surprised myself to feel a little lighter for it.

"Thanks, Pops," my boy murmured, and instead of tucking it immediately into the inside of his own jacket, he cracked the lid, let out a heavy breath, and opened it up the rest of the way to look at the set.

I didn't look. Instead, I took a hearty sip of the tequila, glad he had brought the good shit out here. It went down with a smooth and sexy burn, whispering the promise of oblivion if I indulged in enough. Maybe later tonight, but not right now. This conversation had been a long time coming and, though it promised to be painful, it needed to happen before anything else.

He clicked the ring box closed and gripped it in his fist. He bounced that fist a couple of times against his lips as he choked up, glancing away and blinking a few too many times to clear the moisture from his eyes. He sniffed, cleared his throat, and turned the conversation back on me asking, "So, what's with the haircut?"

"Well, like I said, I went and saw your mother early this morning."

He stared at me intently, cocking his head to the side and asked, "Did she have something to say or was it just the smell of roses?"

It'd happened to both of us, but it was still uncomfortable talking about it. We didn't subscribe to mystical mumbo-jumbo bullshit, but what went on with Tilly, after she was gone, was too strong for either of us to really ignore. For Dray, it'd happened a few times. The one time it'd happened to the both of us at the same time had been when Everett had given birth to their boy. Dray had come out of the delivery room grinning like a fool, crying 'It's a boy!' and as soon as his eyes had fell on me, his expression had changed and I knew he smelled it, too. The overpowering perfume of his mother's favorite roses had descended on the both of us like a cloud.

No one else had said anything about it, but for us it'd been so strong, choking, cloying, and so full of pride and joy it wasn't about to be ignored by either of us. We'd talked about it late that night in Evy's hospital room, Dray holding his boy, both the baby and his mama fast asleep. That'd been the last time we'd talked about it until now.

"A little bit of both," I confessed.

"That doesn't explain the haircut. Mom would be pissed if you cut your hair."

I nodded. "Well, I wasn't the only one at the cemetery this morning."

He raised an eyebrow, "Oh, yeah?"

I told him about Marcie and he listened quietly. He sipped his tequila and stared off into the distance, calculating for a bit.

"What are you thinking?" he asked. "That fixing her worldview on Cell and making her feel like she isn't some kind of murderer, or whatever shittin' thing she has in her head, is somehow going to tip the scales back in your favor with the universe?"

I shook my head. "No, just hate seeing another human being hurt over that asshole."

"Pops, why you let this woman cut your hair, of all things? Couldn't you just go talk to her?"

I stared at the licking flames, the crackle and pop of the burning wood filling the silence that stretched between me and my boy, and I confessed, "I think I'm lonely, Son. What's more, I think your mother knows it."

"How's that?"

I shifted, uncomfortable with poking at these feelings, like they were a sleeping bear. I cleared my throat, and unable to hold off anymore, went for my pack of smokes. Dray watched me, patient, while I lit one up and took a deep drag off it. I let my lungs fill with smoke and plumed the air with it on a harsh exhale and told him the rest. About smelling the roses, about the compelling feeling like I should go and see what the fire-hair's deal was.

He nodded and said, "Don't get me wrong, I love Mom and I honestly can't picture you with anyone else but..." It was his turn to let out a harsh breath and he downed the rest of his tequila in one hard swallow. "I think it's time. It's pushing nine years, going on ten. Maybe it's time."

I chuckled and shook my head. "I'm not planning on tapping that ass like a club-girl or hell, even wanting anything romantic – but a friend-ship might be nice, that's all I'm saying," I said.

I thought back to those keen blue eyes staring into mine in the mirror at her station and didn't know if I was a liar right then or not. She had some spark under what had her shook up. I half wondered if, like Tilly, that meant her temper would flare.

I frowned slightly and polished off my own glass of tequila, immedi-ately admonishing myself that comparing the two women was a bad idea, a slippery slope, and that I just shouldn't do it. It wasn't fair. Period.

"You don't need my permission, Pops, but if you came looking for it, you got it," my kid said gently. "You can't change the past, all you can do is work your ass off and build a better future. Not just for this club, but for yourself." He laughed a little and bowed his head. Sweeping his chin length hair behind his ear, he said, "Look around, Pops. The club is doin' just fine. We're all set, we're good. If anything, you need to focus on you now."

"Your mama would be damn proud of you, boy," I said a bit incredu-lously. Again, my son shook his head.

"She only got me the first sixteen years; it's been all you for the last nine or ten, and the shit we've been through in that time? She got the boy ready, you shaped the man. I'm proud of you, Pops. Of how far you've brought us all."

"I destroyed us in the first place, son."

"Maybe, but you didn't wallow and you didn't quit. You rebuilt us; better, stronger. That counts for something, Dad."

"Pour me some more of that fuckin' booze, boy."

He obliged and poured me some, a shit-eating grin on his face as he asked, "What, you getting choked up?"

"Fuck you," I muttered before taking a mouthful, and he chuckled deeply.

"I love you, Pops."

"Love you, too, son."

Silence filtered between us and he asked, "So, you going to see this woman again?"

"Honestly, I don't know. I was kind of thinkin' about leaving it up to fate, but it doesn't seem right leaving her to drown in guilt. *Especially* over Cell."

"Agree with you there, that dude was bad news. I hate to speak ill of the dead – especially a dead brother, but that guy?" He raked his bottom lip between his teeth and I waved him down.

"It weren't for Blue, he wouldn't even have lasted as long as he did," I said unhappily.

There was no changing Cell. He was born wrong. We all knew it. Moreso when his folks and his sister came. They'd been gracious, and grateful that we'd buried him proper, given him the service every brother got.

But I got the impression they were *relieved* he was gone and even more relieved they didn't have to pay for it – which would have been financially crippling to them.

The stories they'd told in hushed whispers, the nervous looks, his sister wanting to see him and make sure he was dead… it was bad.

He'd been a true sociopath. Barely a step off from a serial killer.

If he hadn't had Blue as his real-life Jiminy Cricket, he would have flamed out a long time ago. Given a few years more, he would have taken Blue down with him, and maybe even Hayley. As it was, they were keepin' a sharp eye on the baby. He was Cell's.

We was all just hoping he wasn't Cell's through and through.

4

Marcie…

It was maybe a couple of weeks later that he walked into my shop again. I looked up from my books where I sat at my small front receptionist wrap, and there he was, standing under the swinging brass bell above the door.

"Back again?" I asked, curious. I hadn't really expected to see him again.

"Wanted to see how your son-in-law fared as much as I needed to get this trimmed up," he said, running a hand through his hair. I felt myself rear back slightly in surprise.

"You remembered about Rich?" I asked.

"Well, not his name. You never told me that. Just that he was married to your daughter, Devon."

"Well, I'll be…" I said with a note of wonder in my voice. I stood up, both surprised and surprisingly tickled that he'd remembered.

"So, how is he?" he asked.

"Well, he had his spleen removed, and some broken ribs. A fractured wrist, and was overall pretty banged-up and bruised, but he's doing all right. Should be going back to work here, soon."

"Yeah? What's he do?"

"Why, he's a county Sheriff's deputy."

I had to say, I rather enjoyed the devilish gleam in his dark eyes and the slow sexy grin that overcame his lips. He dipped his chin and chuckled deeply, "Is that right, now?"

"It surely is," I said, and opened up the swinging gate so that he could come back into the salon.

"Yet you still serve the likes of me, eh?" He looked me up and down and stepped through, the tread of his motorcycle boots heavy on the linoleum floor. He shrugged out of his jacket and I looked him in the eye, boldly.

"Honey, I don't care about that. I don't turn no one away from here. It's not who I am." He raised his eyebrows and nodded slowly, and I noticed he'd changed his facial hair. Instead of an unkempt beard, he'd trimmed it down some, taming it, in line with what I'd already done to his hair.

It was hot, and for a moment, I honestly felt like I should be too old to be thinking such thoughts now that I was a grandma – or about to be. Then I dismissed that thought; I was who I was, which was a red-blooded American woman. If I thought the man was attractive, then that's what I thought about him. I could think what I wanted, didn't mean I had to act on it. Didn't mean I had to share those observations, either.

Unfortunately for me, he must have seen it written all over my face, because he asked me, "You like what you see, sweetheart?"

I didn't give him the satisfaction of blushing, but rather answered boldly, "I do believe I do. I like what you done with your beard. Looks nice."

He grinned and hung up his jacket, taking a seat in my stylist's chair, and said, "Why, thank you. I'll take that for the high praise it is, coming from a professional and all."

"You do that," I said. "You just want cleaned up around the edges, then?" He nodded and I put a drape on him, tucking his collar and fussing over it when it didn't like to cooperate.

"Marcie, I'd like to ask you somethin'," he said, as soon as I had wrestled his collar into submission. I glanced up into the mirror above my station and his coal-black eyes caught mine with that burning intensity they had.

"Well, what is it? I ain't got all day," I said with a smile.

He grinned at me and chuckled before he said, "How'd you like to come have a drink with me after this?"

I cocked my head and thought about it a minute before I said, "How you know I ain't got another client after you? That I ain't just fittin' you in?"

"You don't," he pointed out with certainty, and I put my hands on my hips.

"Now, how do you know that?"

"Truth between us?" he asked.

"No, lie to me," I said dryly, feeling like my old self, and swatting him playfully on the shoulder.

"No, now I mean it. Truth between us. I don't do secrets and lies if I can help it."

I raised an eyebrow, the hair on the back of my neck standing up, and nodded finally, "Well, go on, then."

"You keep your calendar online. I had one of my men hack into it, which is how I knew your afternoon was free and you was just hoping for some walk-in's."

I felt my jaw drop open and a shocked little "Ah!" came out of my mouth. I closed it and shook my head.

"I suppose you know it's all kinds of illegal, hacking into someone's personal business like that."

"By citizen's rules, sure, but I ain't no citizen. We live and die by a whole different set of rules."

"So I gathered," I said dryly. No judgment. I knew how things were. I weren't stupid. I gestured for him to get his ass up and head for the shampoo bowl. "But if you want to know something like that, all you have to do is pick up a phone and call me. It's much easier that way."

"Is that your way of giving me permission to call you?" he asked slyly.

I gave him a tight-lipped little smile and yanked his chain some.

"If you can find the number."

He laughed then, outright, and it was a good sound, that ended in a not-so-good one when his chest rumbled with phlegm and he coughed.

"You should quit while you're ahead with that smokin', you'll live longer," I said simply, as he leaned back into the bowl so I could wet his hair.

"Yeah, yeah," he said. "You sound like my wife."

"Sounds like she was a smart lady," I mused.

He chuckled again and said, "She was. She also put up with a fuckton of my shit that she didn't have to."

"Sounds like she was a devoted wife," I said.

"She was that, my Tilly."

I let him lapse into silence while I worked my fingers through his hair, massaging his scalp and lightly scratching it with my nails. He looked fairly serene while I worked, except for an ever-present tightness around his eyes. I couldn't say precisely what it was from, but it was most definitely there.

I took my time and spoiled him a little, washing his hair twice and conditioning it a couple, too. when I finally had him sit up, he seemed a little more relaxed than when he'd come in. He looked a sight, going back to my chair with a towel turban on his head, but it didn't detract from his virile masculinity one bit. It was hard for a man to pull that off, but he did it.

I barely trimmed him up, there really wasn't that much of a need to after only a couple of weeks. I thought it was kind of sweet he came back so soon, the haircut obviously being just an excuse. He seemed a bit twitchy this time, fidgety and having a hard time sitting still. I rolled my lips together and bit them between my teeth in an attempt to suppress my smile. He coughed and cleared his throat and I glanced at him in the mirror. He was trying to keep himself from laughing, and it was adorable. Took me all the way back to feeling like a nervous teen all over again, which, wasn't that funny at my age?

"So, you gonna answer my question?" he finally asked, breaking first, and I let my grin escape its prison.

"What question? I don't remember any question," I said playfully, and he chuckled again and bowed his head.

"You know, you're right about one thing," he said, but didn't elaborate.

I rolled my eyes and asked, "What's that?"

"You really can't bullshit a bullshitter."

I laughed myself and mock-slapped his big shoulder with my finger-tips. I nodded finally and said, "Touché, and I would love to. I actually didn't have any plans."

"Well, all right, then," he said, and let me finish him up. I dusted him off and dried the rest of his hair, using the blow-drier to get as much of the hair slivers off of him as I could. Satisfied I'd done my job right, I whisked off the hairdresser's cape and turned him loose. He stood and leaned forward, getting a closer look in the mirror, and smiled.

"You done me good, woman."

"As if there was any doubt!" I rolled my eyes again, and he chuckled again, and I liked the easy banter we managed. It was light and refreshing. I guess I hadn't realized how lonely I'd let myself get. Not that I was really alone, what with my girls in-and-out all of the time. But I couldn't deny, something was missing for me. A companionship, almost. Although I didn't think half the town, or even the ladies at my church, would be okay with me taking up with a Sacred Heart for company.

Fuck them anyhow I thought and went about sweeping up, while he donned his jacket with the colorfully-patched leather vest over it.

He peeled off some bills and held them out. I waved him off and he scowled.

"Take it, you didn't charge me the first time and I felt bad enough about it."

"It's too much!" I cried, looking at the wad of bills.

"Bullshit, I tip what I want. Now take it."

I took it; his tone brooked no argument, and besides, I needed the money. There weren't no denying *that*.

"Thank you," I murmured, and put it away in the cash drawer.

"How long y'think it'll take you to close this place up?" he asked.

"Twenty minutes or so," I hazarded.

"Okay, I think I'll have me a smoke. I'll meet y' out front."

"All right," I drawled. I went to work, getting everything to its place and counting the day's earnings. I was shorter than what I'd like for a day's work, but it was all right this time; I had a full day's work ahead of me tomorrow, all the little old ladies getting their hair did for church on Sunday. Saturday was my best day, typically, and I hadn't had one off in years. Usually, Fridays were pretty busy, too, but today the bus from the retirement home had broke down and so some of my usual customers hadn't come in.

I closed up shop, put the night's deposit in my purse and took down my denim jacket from the coat-tree by the door. I switched out the lights, set the alarm, and went out front of the shop, sticking the key in the lock and turning it.

My salon was sort of out-of-the-way, around a mile-and-a-half outside of town. The building was an old depot with a filling station attached, though the filling station was long gone. It was somewhat in disrepair, but in that country-chic kind of a way. It was around halfway between town and my house so it worked for me and it worked for the owner of the building, too. I couldn't complain; the rent was cheap. I shared the building with a country gift store and café, and the overhang where the old service station used to be was a year-round outdoor farm stand that only closed for a few weeks during the deepest winter.

Dragon watched me, leaning against the saddle of his motorcycle, smoke curling from a nearly-spent cigarette between his index and middle finger. He took a final drag off it, pinched it between his finger and thumb, and ground it back and forth, the coal and tobacco falling in among the gravel of the front lot. He dragged a boot across the smoking ember and was nice enough to put the spent butt in his pocket rather than dirtying up my parking lot with it.

"Your chariot awaits," he said, and held out a helmet to me.

"Oh, I thought I would just follow you…" I said, and he flashed that mischievous grin at me.

"Ain't scared, are yah?" he asked and I felt myself stand a little taller.

"Now if I ain't scared of the likes of you, what makes you think I'm scared of a little ol' motorcycle?" I demanded.

He chuckled and raised the helmet just a little higher.

I took it and put my purse strap across my chest. He smiled at me a little bigger and reached out to work the unfamiliar strap under my chin.

"Where's yours?" I asked and he grinned.

"Honestly, I didn't expect you to say yes."

I laughed and he put a black bandana on over his head and swung a leg over the front of his ride saying, "Get on, and hold on, sweetheart. I'm gonna take this slow."

"I been on one before."

"Oh, yeah? How long has it been?"

"Oh, hell, going on thirty-some-odd years. I must have been a teenager."

"Well, wouldn't that be more like forty-some-odd years, then?"

"Oh, you!" I could have killed him. He laughed and fired it up. "You're buying just for that," I declared, getting on behind him.

"I do believe *I* asked *you* for drinks. Call me old-fashioned, but that means I was buyin' anyways. Now, what did I tell you about holding on?"

I put my arms around his waist and bit my lips together when I felt a bit of a rush of enjoyment. I mean, he was a lot harder than I'd antici-pated around the middle, which was a pleasant surprise.

Oh, get a grip, Marcie! This isn't a date-date. Who the hell knows what this is, but it surely isn't that.

"Okay, here we go!" he called and pulled out onto the two-lane high-way, pointing us in the direction of the center of town. I held on, but he took it easy on me, something I was secretly grateful for. Pretty quickly, I realized that it would actually be nice to go a little faster, but of course, me being me, I had to be ornery about it.

"You ride like a grandma all of the time?" I yelled over the wind, and the vibration of his laugh tickled me pink all over again.

"Be careful what you wish for, sweetheart!" he yelled back, and twisted the throttle. The bike shot forward, the pavement blurring into a smooth, uniform gray beneath us, and I laughed, delighted.

Of course, that was short-lived because a patrol car pulled out behind us from one of the country sideroads, the blue lights on top lighting up, the siren giving an ominous clipped-off wail. Dragon eased off the gas and slowed, ordering me to hold on tight with a grunt as he pulled off onto the gravel shoulder.

"Ah, damnit," he muttered and I raised an eyebrow. I figured he was used to getting pulled over, and a quick check of the side mirror confirmed that I knew the deputy coming up on us.

Before he had a chance to open his mouth, I called out to him, "Now, Jimmy Hudgins, what in the world are you stopping us for? I know it weren't speeding; I saw how fast we were going."

"*Mama Marcie?*" Jimmy cried, astonished.

"Close your mouth, boy. Golly! Y'act like y'never seen me before, when you were just at my table not two nights ago."

"Yes ma'am, I know, sorry about having to stop you..." he faltered, frowning a bit before putting on his stern deputy's face, which just looked comical to me. "Sir, I'm going to need to see your license and registration, please."

"What for?" I demanded.

"Well, ma'am –"

I stopped him cold.

"Boy, don't you 'Ma'am' me!"

"Yes, Mama," he said, chagrined, then cleared his throat, "I'm stoppin' you on account of…" he faltered a moment, his eyes bouncing between me and the colorful patch on Dragon's back, then back to me, like he was tryin' to say somethin' without sayin' it, and boy, let me tell you, I was havin' none of it.

"Go on!" I barked.

"Well, Kentucky has helmet laws, don'tcha know! It's not safe for your… er… your…"

"Friend." I supplied.

"Yer friend to be ridin' around without one."

"Boy, he is a grown-ass man! And the reason he don't have a helmet on is because it's on *my* head. Shouldn't you be out catching real criminals instead of pushing choices on a feller that is old enough and wise enough to make decisions for his self?"

"Mama Marcie, I'm just doin' my job, now. Don't you interfere, I understand he is your…"

"Friend," I supplied for him again.

"Yes, *friend*, but the law's the law and he must obey it."

"Here you go, officer," Dragon said, a mite too politely, and he handed over his papers to Jimmy, who looked flustered as could be.

"Right, I'll be right back…"

He went back to his car before I could yell at him again and Dragon's shoulders hitched in silent laughter.

"Yer a real Steel Magnolia, ain'tcha?" he asked.

"Well my hair just had to match my personality, don't you know not to cross a ginger?" I asked.

"Yes, ma'am, known quite a few gingers in my time."

"Well, that should have been your first clue," I declared.

"I'm not sayin' nothin'," he said.

I grinned.

"Well, look at you! Smarter than you look, ain'tcha?"

He broke down and couldn't *stop* laughing after that, and I grinned, a little smug and more than a little self-satisfied. I liked bringing people joy, and despite my own unhappiness, I was happy to relieve his. It somehow lessened some of my own. I glanced back over my shoulder at Jimmy, who I loved like a son I didn't have, and felt a little bit guilty about even being unhappy.

I had two beautiful daughters, and even though I had divorced him for hurting me as deeply as he did, my ex-husband was around and would help me at the drop of a hat if I needed it. My son-in-law was great, too and their friends, like Jimmy, had been adopted like they were my very own kids.

I had so much to be happy about, I was so blessed, yet I still felt empty sometimes; lonesome. Because I didn't have anybody to really share it with… and because I'd taken that man's life, even by accident, and took the person that he was from the people that loved him most. I felt another stab of guilt for a very different reason.

Just what the hell was I playing at, being on the back of this bike, with this man, one of the man I'd killed's friends?

I was just about to tell Dragon I'd made a mistake accepting his offer to go for a drink. I was just about to get off the bike and give him back his helmet and have Jimmy give me a ride back to my salon and my car parked out back, but suddenly there was a crunch of gravel behind me and Jimmy was back handing Dragon his papers.

"Now, I shouldn't let you off with just a warning, Mr. Trujillo – "

I giggled at the way Jimmy butchered Dragon's legal last name. He pronounced it 'true-jill-oh.'

Dragon simply grunted, didn't bother to correct him, and put his papers back in his wallet saying, "Thank you kindly, officer. My wallet certainly appreciates it."

"If it weren't for Mama Marcie, I'd be issuing a citation," he said, and I knew he was only half-kidding; Jimmy was a good kid.

"See you for dinner on Sunday," I told him, and he grinned at me, sheepish.

"Yes, Mama."

He went back to his cruiser and got in, and Dragon started the motorcycle back up. Jimmy pulled past us with a wave and Dragon and I carried on, into town.

I smiled, proud of myself at managing some mischief, but in the back of my mind I had to worry a bit. I was pretty sure word would get back to my daughters, Devon and Dylan, at the drop of a hat.

5

Dragon...

Hoo-boy, she had a way about her. I was surprised at the fire she held inside. She hadn't seemed the type when we'd met. I'd been back to visit my wife and the last time, I'd talked about the lady that done my hair, and the smell of roses had been so overpowering it'd been damn near dizzying. I had to think my wife approved, and that mattered to me. It mattered to me a whole lot.

Either that, or I was sliding nose-first into some kind of dementia or Alzheimer's. Which, if that were the case and I ever got diagnosed proper with it, I'd be suck-startin' my forty-five in short order. That there was the one thing I feared as a man: losing my fuckin' mind for real. I wouldn't do it. I'd rather my boy clean up my loss of brains *outside* my skull than any other way. That there was no way t' live and I wouldn't fuckin' do it.

I pulled the bike up to the curb in front of The Spot on the town's old main drag and looked down the block and across the street towards the neon lights in the window of Trig, Rev, and Disney's tattoo shop. I was surprised to find I was nervous about the boys spottin' me with Marcie and I had to ask m'self why that was. It bore lookin' at, but not right then. Right then, I do believe I had promised the lady on the back of my bike a drink.

I shut off the engine and gave the handlebars a light twist as I heeled down the kickstand and leaned the sleek machine onto it. Marcie had gotten off and stood off to the side, up on the curb, where she worked at the unfamiliar strap under her chin with clumsy fingers, trying to sort out how to get the lid off her short, copper hair. I chuckled and went to her rescue.

"Thank you," she said as I lifted the brain bucket off. Her fingertips immediately went to her hair, where she fussed with it until she felt it was presentable enough. I stuck out my arm, the gentlemanly thing to do, and guided her in through The Spot's front door and into the gloomy interior of the bar. It was only slightly dimmer inside than out with sun setting, the late afternoon dragging on into evening on me.

"You hungry?" I asked her, and she said, "Y'know, I am."

I smiled and gave a wave over in Mac's direction. The bar's owner gave me a chin-lift and I pointed out a booth. He nodded, and I headed that way.

"I take it you're a regular," Marcie said and I smiled.

"Naw, Mac and I just go way back," I said.

"Well, that sounds like a story as good as any to start with," she said as I held her hand and she slid into one side of the booth I'd picked. She lifted her hand from mine and raised her eyebrows expectantly while I did the math to make sure the statute of limitations was up on some of the things I'd done to help Mac out back in the day. Of course, there weren't no statute of limitations when it came to murder, so I wouldn't be talking none about *that*.

"You remember how I said that I'd always tell the truth when it came to anything between you and me?" I asked, sliding across the green vinyl bench seat, across from her.

"I surely do," she said with a smile. She had lines around her mouth, deep brackets that made your eyes go to those shell pink lips of hers. She had a nice mouth, which was probably an odd thing to say about a woman but it didn't make it any less true. I enjoyed her smile for a handful of seconds because my next words might potentially wipe the smile off her face.

"There'll be times, like now, I'm gonna ask you if you really wanna hear the truth outta me about some things. I have a past I ain't much proud of, but it's where I came from and I can't change it. All I can tell you about that is I *am* a changed man and that life? It ain't what I'm about anymore. Still, I won't hide what I done if I can help it."

Her smile, as I predicted, faded. She leveled so-serious light blue eyes at me and asked, "You always such a downer, Mr. Dragon?" Her voice was only half serious, a sparkle of mirth remaining in her gaze as she considered me.

"I'd like to think I'm not, but truthfully? Probably, yeah."

"Well, let's start with something simple, then. When did you and Mac over there first meet?"

I chuckled, "In high school, probably sophomore year. I had a thing for his sister, a freshman. He bloodied my nose over it."

"Well now that's not so bad, now is it? You become friends after that?"

"Hell, no!" I laughed. "We hated each other. I fucked his sister twice before the year was over and she ended up getting knocked up by some other guy the year after that."

I'd taken Cecile's virginity, but she'd been all for it. She'd turned into the school's slut all on her own, though. That weren't nothing to do with me. Neither was the meth habit she'd developed. That'd been all Bobby Fletcher's doing.

"Oh, my! So how did you end up becoming friends, then?" she asked and leaned an elbow on the table, depositing her chin in her upturned hand.

"Well," I cleared my throat some. "That's where the illegal bit comes in. Y'see, Mac was drunk as fuck and his sister was deep into a bad meth habit. He come over to pick a fight with me. Declared it was my fault she ended up the way she did. We got into a hell of a fist fight. He lost, ended up in a heap spittin' blood and teeth, and started cryin' about it. Ended up payin' me to deliver a worse beat-down to his sister's dealer. I did it fer him. We sort of became strange friends after that."

"His sister get help?" she asked, glancing over in Mac's direction.

"Nope. She died. Meth habit ate her alive. Mac raised her kid. Boy's a damn good rancher next county over, now. Earned his way up bein' some kinda rodeo star."

I didn't tell her that, at the time, I'd taken Mac's money but the beat-down I'd served Cessy's dealer hadn't been any kind of altruistic on my part. I'd pretty much planned on runnin' the motherfucker up outta my town, anyhow. He'd been fuckin' with my client base with that new shit. He needed gone. I'd beat his ass into a three-month coma. Of course, I was smart about it and there weren't no trace leadin' back to me.

Cessy'd gotten better for a time, but eventually she'd fallen right back in it. By then we'd moved up in the world from small-time to runnin' guns and workin' for the cartel and I could give a shit about the smaller meth operations.

I didn't delve into those kinds of details, though. Marcie needed to know what kind of man I was, sure. She didn't need to know *every-thing*, though.

"So a sad but somewhat happy ending. Mac's nephew ended up alright and had Mac there for him. Bittersweet, but I guess you can't know how sweet something is until you've had the bitterness to show you."

"That's quite the philosophy," I said.

"Well, I preach a whole hell of a lot better 'n I listen," she said, with a laugh.

"I think that's probably true of most folks," I said.

She nodded.

"That may be."

We didn't say much as Mac drew up to the end of our table with a couple of menus in hand.

"Dragon," he drawled.

"Mac," I gave a nod.

"Usual?" he asked.

I gave another nod. "Sounds good to me."

"An' fer th' lady?"

"The lady'll have an Old Fashioned if you don't mind," she said before I could even ask.

Mac realized his error but didn't apologize, instead he just politely said, "Not at all, ma'am. Be right back with those drinks while you settle on some food."

"Thanks, Mac," I said, and he dipped his chin and lumbered off back towards the bar. I'd helped him out in more ways over the years and we were good now, not close friends by any means, but friendly.

"So what's good here?" she asked, browsing the menu.

"To be honest, it's all good. Mac runs a damn fine kitchen."

"Not especially helpful for narrowing it down for me. What d' you usually get?"

"Burgers are good; real good. I think I'll have me one of them."

"Sounds good," she said and set her menu aside. I set mine aside without really looking at it. Not that I could read it without my glasses, anyways. I knew what was on it. I'd become a frequent flyer at The Spot since all the girls pretty much had homes of their own with the guys and were spending less time at the club these days.

"So, what about you?" I asked her, curious.

"What about me?" she asked.

"Well, what d'you like to do, other 'n hair?"

"Well, I love to read. In the summer time, with a big ol' glass of sweet tea, but in the winter, I like my tea hot."

"Well, we got somethin' else in common, then. I'm quite the reader myself."

She laughed lightly and said, "You probably don't read the same authors I do," she said.

"Into romance?" I asked.

"That I am, and mystery. Love a good mystery, too."

"One of my men has been reading them there romance novels. His woman read them a lot before she died. I think it's a way for him to stay connected to her. He's always got one of her old paperbacks in his hands. He'd probably be the better one to talk over 'em with. I've been known to indulge in a mystery or two. Who's yer favorite author?"

"Oh, well, my favorite author right now is Timber Philips. She doesn't write mysteries, though. She's a romance writer."

"Ain't she a big-name author? The one puttin' out all the movies?"

"She is!" she cried, delighted and her smile was a nice one. I was beginning to realize that Marcie didn't smile a whole lot. At least, not genuine smiles that reached her eyes and touched her soul.

I asked her, "So, what's yer favorite book by her?"

"Oh, that would have to be *Hunter's Choice*."

Tricia, one of the waitresses, looking a little harried and probably late for work, rushed up with our drinks on a tray and stopped the conversation.

"Sorry!" she said, hastily. "Having one of them days." She laughed a little and whipped out her order pad from her apron which was crookedly tied around her slim hips. She couldn't have been older than twenty-one. Just legal enough to even be in here.

"That's alright, Darlin'. We was just talkin', we ain't miss nothin'."

"Thanks for understanding, what can I get y'all?" she asked.

I let Marcie order first and then ordered m'self. Tricia wrote everything down and took the menus from Marcie, who held them out with a polite smile.

"Thank you, I promise to get your food to y' while it's still hot."

"Thank you," Marcie said, taking a sip of her Old Fashioned. I took a sip of my beer and gave Mac a little side-eye for havin' it brought to me in a glass. He gave me a shit-eating grin and a tip of his chin, and I smiled and shook my head. Bottle was just fine by me, never understood dirtyin' a perfectly good clean glass. I was bettin' this was Mac's commentary about bein' out with a woman my own age. It wasn't somethin' that happened – ever.

"So, this *Hunter's Choice*, what's it about?" I asked when Tricia had left and the dust from her whirlwind appearance had settled.

"You seriously want me to tell you what it's about?" she asked and I could see she was taken aback.

"I asked, didn't I?"

"Well, all right, then!"

She told me all about it, all right. By the time she was done, I actually found myself wanting to read it. She was so enthusiastic about it, it was kinda infectious.

The dinner was good, the conversation was better, and what felt like too soon, I had to take her back to her car and say goodnight. I did, but I wished we could have talked longer. It was nice. A nicer time than I'd had in a while. I watched her get into the Honda and waited until she started it up and put it in reverse before I put my own bike in gear and rode off. And no, I didn't kiss her. It wasn't like that.

Though, I'd be a liar if I said the thought hadn't briefly crossed my mind.

6

Marcie…

"Mama!" Devon cried, and when I rounded from my sink full of dishes, her face was white as a sheet and horrified. I frowned and stared at her for half a second, my mind tripping over itself as to what could be wrong, when Jimmy tried to cross unobtrusively behind my pregnant daughter.

"Jimmy Hudgins!" I cried. "You gossip worse than the little old ladies at my salon."

"No, Mama! You do not turn this 'round on him! What were you thinking?"

"Devon," I said, propping one hand on my hip. "Now, I know you're about to become a mama all on your own, but that does not mean you get to mama *me*. I brought you into this world, so I'd like to think I'm ahead of you on the curve. So you just slow your roll there, sweetheart."

Her jaw dropped open, her eyes welled up, and I started to turn back to my sink full of dishes but stopped. "Jimmy! You get in here and finish these dishes, now, since you're seen fit to try an' dirty up my Sunday dinner with a bunch of gossip."

He came into the kitchen as I went to console my weepy, pregnant daughter. I let out a gusty sigh and hugged her and said, "Now, now. It ain't nothin' but them hormones gettin' you going. Honey, I am fine. I cut the man's hair, and he asked me out to dinner. It gets lonely 'round here durin' the week and I didn't much feel like just cookin' for myself, so I wasn't about to pass up a free meal."

"But he's a Sacred Heart!" she wailed.

"So? What they done to you?" I asked.

"Well... well nothing, but Mama! They're criminals! Dangerous ones."

"She's right, Marcie," my son-in-law said gently from the dining room table, his arm still in a sling from his accident.

"Wasn't but a couple of years ago one of their women got killed in their clubhouse. Some beef between them and another MC tryin' to move in on their turf."

I raised an eyebrow and said, "How come I didn't hear anything on the news?"

"Yah don't hear everythin' on the news, y'know," Jimmy said from the sink.

"Seems to me, something like that shoulda made it."

"It was the same day as that plane blew its engine over Florida," my other daughter, Dylan, said, getting up from the table herself and coming over to me and Devon. "It was on the news, you just missed it."

"How the hell could you remember that?" I asked, astounded.

"Dunno, Mama," she said with a shrug. "I just do. Devon's right, so is Jimmy."

"And me. What am I, chopped liver?" Rich, Devon's husband, called from the dining table.

I rolled my eyes, "Really, it's fine! He's just a… a friend."

"And does he know you killed his man?" Jimmy asked from the sink.

"Jimmy!" Dylan scolded, and I moved some of her long blonde hair back off her shoulder and shook my head.

"Don't yell at the man for talkin' the truth," I told her gently. "And yes, Mr. Busy-body. He does know. That's how we met, in the cemetery where I went to pay some respect."

"When'd you go and do that?" Devon asked, mopping at her tears and runny makeup with her sleeve.

I slapped her hand down and handed her the dishcloth off my shoulder.

"Ruin a perfectly good blouse doing that," I scolded.

She laughed and took the dish towel and did things proper. It needed to go in the washing anyway.

"The mornin' after Rich was in his accident," I told them. "Really, y'all are makin' a mountain outta a mole hill. He came in later that day for a haircut and that was that." I huffed out a frustrated and impatient breath. Honestly, I didn't much like explaining myself to a bunch of kids. Even if they weren't kids anymore.

"Just be careful," Dylan said and her brow furrowed in worry.

I smiled. I had to. I loved my girls more than anything and I didn't want them sad or worried for me.

"I'll be fine, y'all worry too much. There ain't been no trouble out of those men since then, has there?"

"Come to think of it, no… just a couple of drunk-and-disorderlies. A bar brawl last year, but it wasn't them that started it."

"See. How you know they ain't turned a new leaf?" I asked, and led Devon back to her seat by her husband. Dylan paced her older sister on her other side and we helped her sit. Girl was seven months pregnant and as big as a house. Bigger 'n I ever got. She was carrying a right big baby. Forget a bun in her oven, she had the whole loaf!

"Men like that don't change, Mama Marcie," Rich said sadly.

"Boys at county *still* talk about some of the things they seen back in the day, when they was at their worst." Jimmy called back to us.

"Oh, like what? How bad could it be?" I scoffed, but the first stirrings of unease started in on me.

"Nothin' that bears repeatin' in front of a lady," Rich declared.

"Shit," I jeered. "You seen that one naked I don't know how many times, and who you callin' a lady? Sure as hell ain't me!" I laughed and Dylan joined me.

"Mama!" Devon cried, aghast.

"Well, it's true!"

"So what if it's true!" Devon's face flamed. "Don't mean it needs talkin' about in mixed company."

"Baby girl, now I know you ain't got yourself fooled into thinkin' he ain't said that much and worse when he's with all them boys at the police station," I said.

Rich wisely kept his mouth shut and I expertly steered the conversation away from Dragon and his motorcycle club. I didn't know what it was, but I didn't want to hear it. Dare I say, I liked the man. He was fun to talk to, and I didn't want to believe he was such a mean cuss. Still, the seeds had been planted by my kid's worry and I started to worry, too.

I wondered if he would talk about it if I just out and asked him. Of course, I didn't even know when I might see him again. Could be tomorrow, could be in a couple of weeks when he just needed his hair cut again. Who knows if he even wanted to see me again? I was likely too boring for the likes of him, anyhow.

I went back and relieved Jimmy from the last of the dinner dishes and he took out my trash without being asked. He was a good boy. Not always real quick, but not dumb by any means. I was hoping for a minute that Dylan would fancy him and they'd take up, but she seemed content to focus on her studies at the local college. Not that I had much to say about it.

When I was her age, I had more than a few wild oats to sow and I had – right up until I got pregnant with Devon. By then, I thought I'd found the love of my life with the girl's dad… turned out the feeling wasn't mutual.

When we got divorced, some ugly words were exchanged, the ones that hurt the worst was the ones where he told me that him marryin' me was only on account of the fact he'd knocked me up with Devon. He apologized about sayin' it later, but what was done was done. I knew the truth of it the moment the words were spoken. There weren't no saving us, just like there weren't no gettin' any of that time back for Bobby.

I sighed, and drained the sink. I suddenly wanted to be alone, to get lost in one of my books where the love and romance felt real. I knew that the time for me to experience any of that true love stuff was long gone and I was more 'n a little bitter about it.

Of course, then all I had to do was look at either one of my girls and that feeling evaporated.

I wouldn't honestly trade any of the years I spent with Bobby if it meant I had to give up my girls. I loved them with the last light my soul had to give. They were just about my everything in this life. I looked at them and felt like even though I may have done things wrong – I did everything just right.

"I hate it when you look sad, Mama," Dylan said and hugged me from behind.

"I know, baby. It comes and it goes." I chuckled. "Just a fact of life, honey, but –my life. I expect you to do much better when it comes to yours."

She sighed and asked, "You want me to stay here tonight?"

"Oh, no, no, no," I said, shaking my head. "You go on and go back to school. I'm sure you got homework to do."

"Yeah," she said kind of sheepishly.

I narrowed my eyes.

"You ain't failing any of them classes, are you?"

"No! No, nothing like that."

"All right, then."

"I love you, Mama," she said, and I turned around from the window we'd watched Jimmy, Rich, and her sister leave out of and gave my girl a fierce hug.

"I love you, too, my girl."

"Just be careful, you promise?"

"I promise. Ain't nothin' gonna happen to me. I'm a tough old broad."

"Can't argue with you there," she said with a devilish grin, and we shared a laugh.

She left, too, and my house that had been so full of laughter and light felt colder and empty now. I sighed and went back to my kitchen to put the whistling kettle on. I fixed myself a big ol' mug of tea and went into my living room to my favorite chair. I made sure my phone was plugged in, so the girls could text me they was home safe and picked up my battered old paperback of *Hunter's Choice*.

I pulled out the bookmark, or 'quitter strip' as I liked to call it, and settled in to read.

My phone buzzed at my elbow and I picked it up, expecting it to be Devon as she and Rich didn't live too far from here. His parents had given their big house to Rich and Devon and had gone and bought a smaller place for themselves when Devon discovered she was pregnant. I smiled, lookin' forward to my first grand baby.

My smile dissolved into a frown when I read the message from an unfamiliar number.

You know, this ain't like no romance I ever read. Not that I ever really read a romance before this.

I felt my eyebrows go up when I realized who it had to be and texted back.

Oh yeah, what'd you expect?

He responded a handful of seconds later.

I dunno, but this wasn't it. Ain't you going to ask how I got your number?

I smiled and bit my bottom lip at the giddy feeling I had.

No. What romance you reading, anyway?

I could almost hear an echo of his deep bass chuckle.

That owl one you was talking about.

I had enough of the texting, I called the number and he picked up on the first ring.

"*Hunter's Choice?*" I asked before he could even say 'Hello.'

"That would be the one, yes," he said, and I could hear the smile in his voice.

"What page are y' on?" I asked.

"Dunno if I got the same copy you do, but I'm on page fifty-four."

I turned forward in my book to fifty-four and skimmed the page.

"Well if it's the same as mine, you're at the part where Jessamine is at the hospital, you just started her chapter."

"Yeah, that would be where I'm at."

"Well, I'll be. I've read it afore, but you've gotten ahead of me from where I'm at now."

"Is that right?" he asked.

"Surely is. So what got you reading that?" I asked.

"You know it was you, but like I said, it ain't what I expected."

"Well, what did you expect?" I asked, suppressing my laughter.

"Not really sure, but this wasn't it. I sure expected a whole lot of fuckin', not a whole lot of actual story."

I laughed and laughed and when I finally got myself together, I said, "Well, the love stories of today are typically written by women for women. They certainly are a far cry from the old Fabio bodice-rippers my mama used to read."

"I can see that," he said. "Found the attack in the barn was done pretty good. Author has a good grip on reality when it comes to violence." I think I paused a little too long, because his voice came back over the line, a little softer, "Marcie, y'okay?"

"Yeah! Yeah, I'm all right."

"Something I said?" he asked.

"Yeah. Y'know, my family was here for Sunday dinner. My two girls, my oldest's husband and his best friend. You recall Jimmy, the deputy that pulled us over?"

"Ah, yeah. I take it they gave y' a hard time about that?"

"They're just worried," I said, and he chuckled, but it held a bitter edge.

"They have a right, goin' by what we used t' be. I done a lot of bad things, gonna take the rest of my life to balance the scales and I still ain't sure it's gonna be enough."

"At least you're tryin'. There are folks out there that do wrong every day of their lives under a false banner of what a good Christian should or would do. I'd honestly hate to be some of 'em when it comes time to meet the maker."

"Mighty strong opinion you got there on the subject."

I sighed. It was, and it wasn't always a welcome one around these parts, but I couldn't stand hypocrisy. I said as much.

"I can't stand hypocrisy, and what kind of Christian woman would I be if God and Jesus can forgive but I can't? I'm aware everybody has a past, Dragon. I'm no different. I just wish that folks nowadays could live and let live a little more. I don't know, maybe I'm bein' naive…"

"Just a bit," he drawled and I had to smile and shake my head. Not that he could see either. "There's nothin' wrong with naivety outta innocence, though. Y' aren't ignorant, not by a long shot."

"I'd like to think not," I said with a snort. "I just want to believe the good in people, least until they do me wrong personally."

"I like t' think that's a noble quality," he said.

"Painful one, for sure," I murmured, which was true. You tended to get hurt a lot with that philosophy.

"I know I'm about to lose points for sayin', but it takes a lot of courage for a woman who's lived as much life as you have – ex-husband, two grown children, grandbaby on the way and the like, to live life that open."

"Was that a crack about my age?" I asked, yankin' his chain some.

"As gentle as I could make it, but yeah. Age has somethin' to do with it."

"I believe you might owe me another drink for that," I said.

There was a long pause and he finally said, "How about next Friday?"

"Can y' make it Saturday?" I asked.

"Y'know, I rightly believe I can."

"Good, pick me up at eight?"

"Eight o'clock at yer place?"

"Yeah, you know where it's at?" I asked. I knew he did. I just wanted to see if he was gonna try and bullshit me.

"Y'know I do, but if I didn't, I could find out."

"Still not quite sure how I feel about that."

"Intimidated?" he asked.

"Yes and no."

"Well that's an interesting answer," he said when I didn't elaborate.

"Isn't it just?" I asked.

He chuckled and said, "You gonna catch up to me?" he asked.

I smiled, "You go on an' read ahead if y' want," I told him. "Don't let me hold y' back."

He laughed again and said, "Maybe, I'm at the point in my life, I could use a little grounding."

"Things stormy?" I asked.

"No, not at all, actually. Just feelin' kind of adrift, while everyone is moored around me."

My heart kind of leapt. It was like he took the words right out of my heart on that one. That's kind of exactly how it felt. I was quiet for a moment while I thought about what he said and finally came to the conclusion that, despite our odd meeting and the circumstances on how we met, I was all right with exploring this a little further and makin' a new friend.

"I know the feeling," I confessed and it felt like a little bit of my silent burden eased.

"I'll see y' Saturday at eight."

"Saturday at eight."

"Night, Marcie."

"Night, Dragon."

The phone disconnected in my ear and I lowered it and saved the number. Sighing, I took a sip of my tea and lifted my book, determined to catch up, and tickled he'd even picked it up.

7

D**ragon…**

I hung up the phone and blew a plume of smoke into the air, leaning back on the swinging bench around the fire-pit. I pressed a hand to the back of my neck and tried to ease the kink I'd put into it out, while I rolled my eyes heavenward. The sky was rich with star-scatter, and I let my mind wander a bit.

"Different, ain't they?"

I jumped and let my breath out slow as Doc trudged the rest of the way up the earthwork to the plateau the fire-pit setup rested on.

I shook my head.

"I may be gettin' older, and I may be tryin' to live peaceful, but it's still a real bad idea sneakin' up on a feller, old friend."

Doc chuckled and dropped onto the bench beside me.

"My bad. Maybe I just been of a reckless kind of mind, lately."

"Miss her?" I asked, knowing right where he was at.

"Seems like more, not less, with every day," he said.

I nodded and felt terrible. I knew how he felt, and I didn't wish that on nobody. Least of all, him. Doc was one of the best of us when we were at our worst. I felt hell over guilty about how we'd practically conscripted him into the club, but at the same time, he'd stayed. Found something with us he wasn't gettin' out there, in his citizen life.

"Stop that," he said, and shook his bald head.

"Stop what?" I demanded.

"Lookin' like I kicked yer favorite dog. As much as y'all dragged me into this life, I'm glad fer it. You kept me straight, for all yer crooked ways," he said with a gusty sigh.

Outta respect for the man and his position as a doctor, I stubbed out my cigarette on the sole of my boot.

Doc had come to us by way of Unkind, who ran a lucrative bookie gig on the side. Club sanctioned, of course. He'd hooked Doc, got him in debt with the club, and when Doc couldn't pay, rather than hurt him, we used him. It was right useful having an on-call emergency physician and surgeon attached to the club.

We could have made his gambling mistake a painful one, but instead, the Vietnam vet found somethin' he'd been missin' since his discharge from the Army. We was surprised when he wanted in, but we saw the benefit. We made him work for it, though. Made him prospect like any other. He'd earned those colors on his back twice over. He paid for 'em in the blood of his woman, and for that, I was heartily sorry.

"Never wanted you to know this kind of pain, Doc."

"I knew it the day she showed up in my ER, D. You can't know how sorry I was – and still am – that I couldn't save Tilly."

"I do know. I can't tell *you* how sorry I am our sins came back to haunt us with Chandra."

"I know you feel responsible, but that ain't how it went down. Those cats brought the fight, we just finished it – just not in time. That there was straight up Karma."

"I know it," I said, shaking my head.

"Speaking of women…"

"Yeah?" I asked.

"What you got going on with this lady?"

"Marcie?" I asked.

"If that's her name. You been playin' this one awful close to the vest, brother."

"I have?" I asked, thinking it over and realizing that, yeah, I had been. I didn't talk about her much, if at all, with any of the boys. I was surprised this was the first I was gettin' any of them askin' about it.

"Huh, I guess I have," I said finally, to fill the silence, realizing too, Doc was using my own tricks against me.

"So?" he asked, when I was silent too long.

"So, she's not what I expected," I said honestly.

"How's that?"

"She's got spunk, that's for sure. Ornerier 'n cat shit."

He laughed at that and shook his head, "Ornerier 'n cat shit? I'm hafta remember that one. Just where do you get this shit?"

I chuckled with him and shook my head, "I dunno where that one came from, but if I had to guess…"

"Tilly," we said in unison.

"She like her?" he asked.

I shook my head, "No. She's different, in just about every way, but no less strong that I can see."

His mouth turned down at the corners and he nodded, mulling it over.

I smiled to myself and said, "I like her, but just as a friend for now. It's kind of nice reconnecting with a citizen and that kind of life. Certainly it's a simpler one than ours."

"Boring, compared to ours," he said dryly, and I cast my eyes back towards the sky and shook my head.

"Maybe once I thought like that, and maybe I'm just gettin' old, but I don't see it so much as boring anymore," I said. "Just different."

"You like her that much?" he asked.

"Naw, man. She's just… different. Calmer. Bein' a grandpa, now, I kind of need calmer. Don't you think?"

He laughed and said, "I think we've all needed calmer for a good long while."

"Truth to that, my brother. Truth to that."

"You done with that?" he asked, and I looked down at the tattered paperback resting on my knee.

"Actually, if you don't mind, I'd right like to finish it."

"Well," he said. "Looks like we can maybe start our very own book club."

I laughed at that and said, "Chandra's callin' us both a pair of pussies, right now. You know that, right?"

"Oh, I know it," he said, his shoulders shaking with laughter. "What I wouldn't give for her to be here so I could rail that pussy of hers."

"Still a few club girls that come around."

He shook his head.

64

"Wouldn't feel right about it."

I nodded. That's where Doc and I differed. When Tilly had died, I'd tapped whatever ass was on offer, hoping to find something. I still didn't know what. I never did, of course, but a man has needs and I had no trouble gettin' 'em met.

"Hey," I called, when he got up to head toward his club room.

He looked back over his shoulder.

"Yeah, what?"

"You got any more by this broad?" I asked.

He nodded, "One of Chandra's favorites. I got a whole shelf of her stuff. Even went out and bought her newest stuff. The stuff that came out after she was gone. I go down to the cemetery and read 'em to her sometimes."

Tilly wasn't much of a reader, or I probably would have done the same. She was a gardener, though, so I brought her roses from her garden, and sometimes left packets of seeds.

"That's a good thing, Doc."

"Yeah?" he asked, his expression sober, so somber.

"Yeah. I'm sure Chandra loves it."

He sniffed and looked at the sky, I pretended I didn't see the tears.

"I miss her somethin' awful, D."

"I know, brother."

"I can't smell her or hear her like you can Tilly."

"I'm sorry," I said. I didn't know what else to say.

"Feel her, sometimes though."

"That's good! That's good, Doc."

He nodded and didn't say anything else. Just turned abruptly and trudged back toward the club's main building and the back door. When the old screen clacked shut behind him, I heaved a big sigh, letting it out slow. I wished I could do something. I was agitated that I couldn't. I pulled out a cig and put it between my lips while I fished for my lighter. I breathed in the smell of roses over the smell of fresh tobacco as I flipped back the lid on my Zippo.

I thumbed over the wheel, the friction against the flint sparking, the cotton wick of the lighter catching. I stared at the flame and murmured around my cig, "I wish I knew what to do for him, baby."

The breeze out here kicked up and whisked the cloying smell of my wife's flowers away. I lit my cig and sucked in a lungful of smoke, my nerves settling as the nicotine hit my bloodstream. It was too dark to read out here, now; the fire-pit was cold and dark. I didn't want to light it. I just wanted to sit out here for a bit, smoke my cigarette, and stare at the sky.

That done, I stubbed it out on the sole of my boot and gave the butt the same treatment I had the first one, flicking it in among the fire setup in the pit to burn off the rest of the way. I heaved my ass up onto my feet, my old injuries protesting, my joints creaking, and decided it was a bit cooler out here than I'd realized.

I went in, the club quiet and dark. Everyone had gone home to be ready for the work week ahead. I liked the club when it was peaceful like this. Still. The halls were thick with nostalgia, and the vibrant energy of parties past was still there, but dulled down until the next shindig could replenish the supply. I went into my club room and kicked the door shut, dropping into my old recliner with a sigh and a creak of leather from my jacket and cut.

I cracked open the novel and picked up where I left off. I wanted to stay just ahead of her if I could. I wanted to be able to talk to her about what happened without having the story spoiled.

I was surprised.

Mysteries that were in the same series, after a while usually got kind of formulaic, but I'd always heard and thought romance was a genre particularly guilty of being cookie cutters, the same ol' shit rehashed from book to book, despite changes to eye color or hair color, to names, or the setting. Guess these really weren't your weird aunt's romance novels. This one had some heart to it. Was different, even if the basis for it was the same. Guy saves girl from the awful things... they fall in love... and ...Happily-Ever-After.

In this one, though, it started out with the girl saving him. Even if she didn't know what or who he was right away.

It was nice. I could see why Marcie liked them. I could also see why Chandra liked them. Tough broad that she had been, she also had a good heart, a soft center. Especially where Doc was concerned.

I always said women had it tougher than any man out there, when it came down to it. That's why I'd been adamant, even at our worst, that women and children were fucking off-limits. They were the ones who had to shoulder the burden of life after men like me were gone. They were the ones that suffered most for our sins.

I tried to push back the guilt and found it was a little easier this time. The smell of roses was faint but welcoming. Tilly was just so *present* lately, and I knew in the bottom of my heart that she was tryin' to tell me to let go. I was a stubborn bastard, though, and if it was one thing I was good at, it was hoarding things. Just like my namesake, I hoarded all sorts of things like treasure. Books, memories, feelings, family, and unfortunately, grudges.

I was *real* good at holding a grudge.

More 'n a few men had ended by my order or my hand, because of a grudge. In the end, it'd come back to bite me, in so many more ways than just my wife's death. I was tryin' to be better at letting things go, but Tilly? I didn't know if I could. I honestly didn't know if I ever should.

I sighed, and pulled my readers off my face, pressing my fingertips into my eyes and tried to deal with the pain. Sometimes the guilt, the hurt, the grief, it welled up outta nowhere as fresh as a daisy, and that echoing sinister voice would snake out of the darkest corners of my mind and remind me what a piece of fuckin' shit I was, how everyone would be so much better off without me, and how I should just eat my gun and get it over with.

Countless times I'd sat here with that very same gun out and resting on my knee, very black against the light denim of my jeans. That voice had grown further and fewer between its appearances, and right now, it was barely a whisper, but like always, when it made an appearance, I contemplated it. I thought it over silently and I thought about all the boys, my son, and now, my grandson.

While I could rationalize that leadership was no longer a problem, that Dray could run this club as good as I could, anymore, I couldn't do that to my boy. I couldn't leave my boy an orphan. Even though he was a man himself, now, he still had a lot to learn and I had to stick it out to smooth his way as best I could. I'd already made life rough enough for him.

Then there was my new daughter. Probably one of the brightest spots of joy in my life, next to my grandson. She'd already had to say goodbye to her real daddy. I couldn't do that to her twice over.

Finally, there was my grandson. I was nostalgic, I admit. I'd taught Dray to shoot, to fish, and to ride. While I would stand back and let him do the same for his boy, I wanted to be there just the same.

They were why I held on, even though I had some rather unique thoughts on the matter of suicide.

I stood up, setting Chandra's copy of *Hunter's Choice* aside and pulled off my jacket and cut. I hung it on the back of the door and stripped down, getting ready for bed, pulling on the pair of tartan flannel pajama pants Everett had gifted me for Christmas.

I picked up the book and took it and my readers with me to the bed, switching on the bedside lamp. I went back over to my chair and switched out my reading lamp with a sigh.

I fell asleep sometime around where the main female character, Jessamine, was arguing with the crotchety old bastard, Charlie, about takin' a seat at the dinner table.

I liked Charlie.

He reminded me of me.

8

Marcie...

I heard him before he was even close to comin' up to my door. I went to the kitchen door and opened it up. My driveway went down the side of my house and spilled into a flat gravel lot outside my kitchen door in what was, technically, my back yard. Kind of hard to miss the sound of a motorcycle as loud as his coming down the drive. It damn near shook the whole house.

"Evenin'!" I called as he shut off his machine. "Does that thing really need to be that loud?" I asked, curious.

He grinned at me and stood, swinging a leg over the saddle and facing me over the back of the sleek bike, all butter-soft leather and shiny chrome. The tank was a glossy black, with the MC's logo airbrushed on the tank under a shiny seal of topcoat.

"Loud pipes save lives, Sugar."

"I suppose I didn't think of that."

"Citizen like you, there's a lot to learn," he said.

I crossed my arms over my chest and scowled, "And just what's *that* supposed to mean?" I demanded. "A 'citizen like me'."

"Now, now," he said, coming around his motorcycle, walking up to my little porch. He propped a booted foot on the bottom step and put his thumbs through his belt loops in front. "Don't mean no harm by sayin' it. It just is what it is. The world I come from is both simpler than yours and a lot more complicated."

I tilted my head and arched a brow, searching his face. I saw it there, in his eyes. The invitation in his smile. I couldn't decide how it made me feel, if it felt open and welcoming, or if it held a more sinister connotation to it...

Come into my parlor, said the spider to the fly...

"Apology, even though it sucked, accepted," I told him, and held my hand out. He laughed and took it, and I descended the three steps like a debutante — not that I'd ever been one. I'd had dreams, but I was far too poor growing up for it to ever happen.

"So, where're you takin' me this time?" I asked and he smiled at me.

"Well, that would ruin the surprise. You gonna lock your door?" he asked.

I shook my head.

"Never have," I said.

"This day and age, you have to be crazy."

"I'm goin' out with a Sacred Heart in this town when my son-in-law is a Sheriff's deputy. Pretty sure if you ain't figured it out by now, I'm way past crazy, sweetheart."

He laughed and nodded, "Touché, beautiful. Touché."

He handed me a spare helmet that he'd had hooked around the back of the backrest thingy on his motorcycle, and helped me fasten it right. I got on behind him and he fired up the machine. I jumped at the noise, but I'd jumped the first time, too. I was like that, very sensitive to loud noises. Always had been, no real reason behind it. I couldn't watch a scary movie for nothin'. I didn't cover my eyes, I plugged my ears. It could be somethin' I'd seen a thousand times, but once that music got started and ramped up, I was done for unless I couldn't hear it.

I couldn't hear a damn thing over the roar of the wind, but then again, it was nice not to. That wasn't the point of riding anyway, I didn't think. Talkin'. Talkin' was reserved for whenever we got where we were goin'. Right now, it was just a nice sunset ride, easing into the thrum of the bike, the rush of the pavement beneath the tires as it ate up miles of highway and the dull roar of the wind rushing over us, carrying what stress and troubles we may have had burdening us away.

I could get used to this goin' for a ride. It was nice. I'd forgotten how much I enjoyed it. We rode out along the parkway away from town and turned off onto some older country roads until he slowed and turned down the drive of one of the racehorse farms in the area. A woman came out the front door of the cabin-like ranch house and skipped lightly down the steps. As soon as Dragon cut the engine, the noise of a saw coming from one of the tin outbuildings nearby could be heard finishing a cut, the blade winding down as whoever used it switched it off.

"There you are! Was wondering when you were going to get here," the woman cried.

"Marcie, I'd like you to meet my niece, Bailey." I smiled and got off the motorcycle and held out my hand. She gripped it firm, but nicely. Her palm was rough with callouses. Despite her well-kept appearance that screamed old money, she wasn't unfamiliar with what real work was about, and I immediately liked her for it. She smiled, her teeth perfect, straight and white, the way only a pair of braces and regular visits to the dentist could make 'em, and I smiled back.

Unlike a lot of Appalachia, I was blessed with good genetics, so while my teeth weren't perfectly straight, they were the ones God gave me and they weren't rotten. I thought it was a funny thing to be thinking all of this, but at the same time the mind wanders where the mind wanders and thankfully, mine wandered from teeth to *What on earth are we doing here?*

I tuned into Bailey talking to Dragon. She was saying, "Saw 'em out at the edge of the north-east pasture the other day. Rush'll take you out there as soon as – ah, there he is."

A man was jogging up to us, sawdust in his hair and in drifts across his broad shoulders, which were covered in a straining black tee-shirt with the Sacred Hearts MC logo on the front where a pocket should be. He slowed up to a walk a few strides away, out of breath slightly, and stuck out a hand to Dragon.

"Yo, D. Was wondering when you would make it."

They pulled each other into a fierce hug and stepped back from each other.

"Marcie, I'd like you to meet my man, Rush."

I felt a fit of nerves fizzle to life in my gut in a flurry of moth's wings against the inside of my stomach. Butterflies were cute and romantic; there wasn't nothin' cute about what I was feelin' right now, though. Not as my thoughts raced about, wonderin' how the woman who murdered this man's friend was about to be received. I didn't say nothin' about it as Rush, brown eyes sparkling under a mop of short, dirty blonde hair, reached out and took my hand. He winked at me, bowed over it gallantly, and smacked a quick kiss across my knuckles.

"Pleasure to meet you, Marcie."

I giggled, the nerves evaporating, the moths exploding into a riot of butterfly wings anyways.

"Well, aren't you a charmer?" I asked. Bailey was lookin' at Rush with fondness and a touch of adoration and I had to smile. It was the same way my daughter and her husband, Rich, looked at each other, and those two had a deep love and respect for one another to the point I knew I didn't have to worry if it would last. I knew it would.

"Bailey tell you we're headed to the north-eastern pasture?" he asked.

"She surely did," Dragon said.

"Alright, let's do it," Rush said with another wink.

"Have fun, you guys; love you, baby. See you when you get back," Bailey said, and with a wave she headed back toward the house.

"I don't even know what we're doing," I said, with a laugh.

"That's the whole point, sweetheart. It's a surprise."

Rush led us over to a beat-up old farm pickup and dropped the back tailgate. He brought down a wood stepstool and set it on the ground and held out a hand.

"Ladies first," he declared and I took his hand and stepped up on the stool like a stair, and put a foot on the back of the tailgate. With a slight groan of protesting old joints I climbed into the back. Dragon climbed up right behind me and we settled in, our backs against the cab of the truck while Rush hefted the stepstool back against the tailgate after he'd shut it, and used a bungee cord to strap it into the back corner of the truck bed.

He patted the side of the truck twice and raised his eyebrows at us, and went around to the driver's seat. I laughed and looked over to Dragon and said, "I'm trusting you aren't about to bury me out the woods somewhere."

He chuckled and shook his head, "You're far too entertainin' to have around, sweetheart. Wouldn't dream of it. You'll see what I'm up to soon enough."

The nerves were back, a mix of butterflies and moths this time, as the truck fired up and we lurched across the uneven ground and turned to go deeper into the horse farm's property.

He had this half-smile on his face in the dying light, one that said he was sure of himself and that I was in store for something special. We would see. I didn't exactly get my hopes up much anymore.

Bobby'd sort of broken me of that habit with Christmas and birthday gifts consisting of a new vacuum cleaner or ironing board.

He'd managed to outdo himself a few times, usually with a big gaudy piece of jewelry, but no matter how much I hinted, he never picked up on the fact I'd love a cozy weekend getaway or a nice dinner for two. I wanted his time, not a new necklace or the nifty new gadget to clean the house with. Hell, I didn't even use the fancy mop he bought me. I always did my kitchen floors on hands and knees, it was the only real way to get it clean.

We turned through a wide pasture gate and bumped and rocked over an uneven field. Just when I was like to think I was gonna go crazy, we stopped and Rush threw open the driver's side door and hollered out, "Just a sec, lemme get the truck gate for you."

He jogged around to the back of the truck and unhitched the footstool while Dragon helped me to my feet. I dusted some stray straw off the seat of my britches as Dragon jumped down and both men held hands up to me to make sure I got down okay.

"Why, thank you, gentlemen," I said, laughing, but the laughter died on my lips when I turned to face the field and the line of trees past it. Sitting just a few feet from us was two low lounge chairs, the outdoor type, handcrafted from some beautiful honey-colored wood, the edges left gnarled and natural, the back and seats planed and sanded smooth.

Between the two chairs, sat a stout matching table. An old camp lantern was on it along with a square cut-glass decanter of some kind of liquor and a pair of matching glasses, just sitting and waiting.

"I'll be," I declared. "What is all this?"

"Right, no cell service out here," Rush said and handed Dragon a little radio. "This has the reach to get me back out here. Just turn it to channel two and call me up when you're ready."

"Will do, Rush. Thanks a million."

"Ain't no thing, Prez. See you later."

"Thank you!" I called back to him, coming to my senses a little late. He grinned and gave a wave in the half-light over the bed of the truck. He turned on the headlights, and made a U-turn in the field before chugging back the way we'd come in.

"Thought you could use a drink and to relax," Dragon said, gesturing to one of the seats. "I know I could use a little peace and quiet."

"You did all this, for *me*?"

"Nah, I did it more for me, I just figured I might like to share it with you." He winked at me and I couldn't tell if he were joking or dead serious.

I went to the seat on the right and sat down. He reached down to the little shelf under the table and pulled out a throw blanket, laying it over my lap.

I laughed lightly and said, "Why, thank you!"

He chuckled, and pulled the stopper gently from the decanter and poured two glasses of what smelled like vanilla bourbon.

"That smells heavenly," I groaned.

"It's not my usual, that's for sure, but I have to agree. Rush 'n Bails outdid themselves."

"What is your usual?" I asked, taking the glass he offered me and closing my eyes, breathing in the rich, warm, and slightly spicy aroma. It held the kind of spice that you'd use in a nice pie or a batch of cookies, warm and fragrant, sweet and lovely. I had to know where they got this bourbon, I needed to use it in my pecan thumbprint cookies come Christmas time.

Dragon set his own glass aside on the armrest of his chair and slung another throw over the back. He shifted the decanter aside and took his lighter from his pocket, lifting the hurricane glass on the lantern to get it going. He kept the flame low for now, the light barely there even as the dark crept out from the woods in front of us.

"We here for the stars?" I asked, curious. Something Bailey had said about 'them' being spotted made me want to fish for information.

"No, just thought it might be nice to listen to the cricket song and relax," he said, but his smile told me he wasn't trying all that hard to lie to me.

"Well, all right, then." He had settled in his own seat, tossing the throw over his legs and I held out my glass to his. He clicked his glass to mine and I said, "To a relaxing evenin' out."

"Here, here," he murmured.

The bourbon was silky smooth with a nice sweet edge across my tongue, warming me all the way down as I swallowed. I sighed happily and leaned back.

"Where'd you leave off in your copy of *Hunter's Choice*?" he asked.

"Oh, ha, I maybe got a paragraph or three in on Sunday night and I fell asleep. I got a little bit further later in the week…" I set my glass down and slipped my readers out of the pocket I kept them in in my purse. "Turn that up a bit, maybe?"

"Sure." He turned the little knob on the lantern and gave it more wick. The flame grew until I could see the book I'd taken out of my purse.

"A bit more?" He obliged and I said, "There." He leaned back in his seat and I checked the chapter heading, saying, "Ah, yeah, I left off not too much further. Chapter sixteen."

"Oh, that'd be one of Jessamine's chapters. That's all you, sweetheart."

"What, you want me to read it?"

"Well, why not?" he asked. "You got me into this mess." And with that, he pulled his own battered copy of the book out of his inside pocket. I laughed and he gave me a sly grin and brought out his own pair of reading glasses. "Next book is my choice, though."

"All right, okay," I said, smiling, buying myself time to get used to the idea. I took a sip of the bourbon in my glass, savoring it a moment. I decided I liked his proposition and said, "That's fair enough, I think." I could barely keep my smile at just a smile. I had to fight it to keep it from becoming a full-blown grin when he had to turn backwards in the book from nearly the ending to get to my same page.

I took a breath and was just about to speak when it happened.

The raucous call of an owl split the spring air and I felt my eyes widen.

Dragon reached for the lamp and doused the light to its barely-there glow, and we stared at one another in the close dark, our ears straining.

It happened again!

Both of us turned our heads and scanned the tree line as the last haunting note drifted on the slight breeze. I lowered my book, slipping the bookmark back into place and stared hard, hoping my eyes would adjust and I caught sight of the magnificent bird as it took wing and glided over the pasture.

I sucked in a sharp breath as it swooped above the ground and then its silhouette, lighter against the night, winged back into the air, wheeling against the starry sky with a mouse or something clutched in its talons. I barely dared to breathe as it took its catch to the nearest fencepost to dine.

"Oh, my god," I whispered and leaned back. Dragon eased the wick back up carefully on the lantern, and the bird, just at the edge of our pool of light, froze. "Don't scare him!" I hissed, but it was too late. Clutching her kill, she winged back to the trees. "Aw, damnit! I think that was me," I said, dismayed. "Shoulda just kept my mouth shut."

Dragon chuckled and said, "They're out there. Bailey says she's got a mated pair in these woods, and there are some barn owls in her barn."

"That is just fabulous!" I said.

We were speaking in low, careful tones and he smiled around the rim of his glass.

Another owl called from the tree line, or maybe it was the same owl. It was hard to tell. I smiled and leaned my head back to listen and murmured, "This here is mighty special. Thank you."

"Gotta find the magic in the simple things," he murmured, and I smiled and rolled my head on my neck to look over at him.

"There's a lot of truth in that statement," I said.

He chuckled and looked over his readers at me the same as I looked over mine at him.

"Where were we?" he asked.

I laughed and said, "Gonna need a little more light than that."

"Your wish is my command."

"Wrong fairy tale, or myth or whatever," I said.

He laughed lightly and said, "Well, I stand corrected."

9

Dragon…

   We'd gone through most of the book, the evening ambling on, the owls calling, the crickets lazily chirping as we read to each other by the lantern's light. I glanced up about half way through one of my chapters to read and found Marcie dozing lightly, a faint appreciative smile gracing her lips.

I stopped and looked over her face.

She was an ageless kind of beauty. Not Hollywood glam, but real. Salt-of-the-earth kind of people. Motherhood, and the kind of person she was, had etched laugh lines gently around her eyes and mouth, her skin was smooth and free of makeup. When her eyes opened, they were nearly colorless by the lantern light, but kind, and the whole effect with her country perfect outfit made her the sort of beautiful you married. Not the kind to hit and quit. She took care of herself, and had a respect for herself that declared that if you didn't take care of her, she'd sure but leave your ass, and it sounded like that was just what she'd done where her ex was concerned.

A shame, too. She really seemed like she was a good woman. Good women almost always seemed to be handed a raw deal. I know it was selfish to think it, but I found myself thinking if I stuck around and treated her right, I might be able to tip my scales some. In fact, I think I'd lost sight of my original purpose after meeting and talking with her, that original purpose being to just convince her that Cell's death really was squarely on Cell's shoulders for riding like a fuckin' idiot that day.

"What?" she asked.

"Just lookin' at you. You gettin' tired?"

She smiled, "I didn't think I was, but I suppose it is gettin' late."

"Say no more," I said softly and cued up the radio Rush gave me and turned it to channel two like he asked. I said into it, "Yeah, Rush, you there?"

The radio crackled to life, "Yeah, I'm here D. Thought you guys were fixing to sleep under the stars tonight. I'll be right out."

"Thanks, my man."

"No problem, I'm out."

I switched it off and returned it to my pocket. Marcie stayed huddled under the throw and I realized it'd grown chilly the more the night had dragged on. She was staring at the skies above us and I turned my attention that way, too.

"Ever wonder if they're up there, lookin' down on us?" she asked, softly.

"Who?"

"Your man, maybe even your wife?"

"Some of my men, sure. My wife? Oh, absolutely. Cell? No way. I hate to speak ill of the dead, but Cell? If he went anywhere, guaranteed he went straight to Hell."

"That's an awful thought," she said, and sounded sad.

"Much as I hate for it to be true, it is," I said. "A very true one." I sighed and it was weighed down with the broken hopes and dreams I'd had of Cell potentially turnin' himself around once he'd come to us. It hadn't taken me long to realize that wasn't gonna happen. He was his own animal.

Hell, he *was* an animal. All the cold calculation of a true-born predator. The absolute pinnacle of the food chain. That man had a mouth so cold, butter wouldn't even melt in it.

I just wished I knew how to explain it, or prove it, to Marcie. I sighed. I knew how, but the trick was going to be gettin' her to agree to it.

"I know it sounds awful," I said when she'd been quiet and reflective too long. "But the God-given truth of it is, Cell was one of the rare ones who was just plain born *wrong*. He didn't have a care for anyone but himself, and he was straight incapable of it."

"He was loved by someone," she said feebly, and I realized I was somewhat gettin' through.

I nodded.

"He was loved by two people, actually. A strange dynamic, for sure, to the rest of us, but by the same token, the fact he was loved by those people wasn't a mark of how good of a man he was. It was sincerely the mark of how good those two are."

"That's quite a thing to say," she said quietly.

I smiled and nodded.

"Someday, I'd really like for you to meet ol' Blue and Hayley. I think they'd like to meet you, too."

"Me? Now, what would they want to meet me fer?" she demanded.

I sighed, "Marcie, you're a good woman. A good woman who is carryin' around far too much guilt over what you think you done. But you didn't do anything, sugar. Cell was ridin' like a right idiot that day. You were just livin' your life. I don't know why the fates picked you, other 'n they may have felt sorry for Cell – which gods know why. Maybe they wanted to ensure at least one person mourned his passing."

"Was he really that bad?" she asked, her mouth agape.

"Worse," I assured her. "No bullshit, there. He was as manipulative and out-of-control as a person could be. Didn't give two fucks about who he dragged to hell with him."

"Then how did he even become a part of your club?" she asked.

"That's a good question," I said. Unfortunately, I didn't have a satisfying answer for myself, let alone for her. I would try to give her what I could, though. I figured I owed her at least that much.

"I don't suppose you know how an MC works, do yah?"

She shook her head. "Not particularly, but I'm always up for learning new things."

"Alright, I'll see if I can't explain this here…" I thought about how to phrase things before I opened my mouth again, and decided to keep it as simple as I could. "So you got an MC, and it's a new one, right? And you get enough guys and other guys start comin' around, interested, and eventually it's grown to a point that you realize that while good, it's gettin' a bit too crowded, and so you start lookin' at expandin' your territory."

"Like the Romans?" she asked, smiling.

I laughed a little. "I guess you could liken it to conquering the world," I said. "So you got a few guys who are good guys, they just don't necessarily agree one hundred percent with the way the club is goin' and so one of 'em comes to you and says, 'Y'know, I got two or three guys that we could go over here and set up a chapter and what do you think?' Next thing you know, one chapter becomes two… And *here's* where it gets interesting."

"Okay," she said carefully.

"You gotta trust 'em, because that's what this whole thing is about. Trusting your brothers to follow the club charter and rules that have been set forth, and to live by 'em.

"So they go off and start their new chapter, but you don't really have too much say in who they bring into it, because the guy you sent out is now a president in his own right?"

"Very good," I said. "And, yes and no. I still got *some* say in overall operations being that I'm the top dawg, but for day-to-day? Not so much. Who they bring on into their chapter, not so much."

"Because you trust them to bring in the right kind of people," she said.

"Very good. I don't suppose I can much fault the guys who brought in Cell; he was a very charming individual. But by the time he made it down this way and joined up with my chapter, it was a little late. He was part of the club."

"You couldn't just kick him out?" she asked.

"Not how this whole thing works, sweetheart," I said, shaking my head. "Short of breaking some very specific rules, once a man is accepted, he's one of us. And you don't turn your back on a man who is your brother so easily. It's sort of the antithesis of the whole fucking point."

She nodded carefully and I searched her face.

"That being said, Cell was on his way Out Bad. It was only a matter of time before he pulled something that couldn't be ignored. All of us saw it coming."

"You seem sad about that," she said softly.

"It's not an easy thing, giving up on one of your brothers. None of us want to do it." I kept it to myself that the real thing that saddened me wasn't necessarily losing Cell, it was the prospect of losing Blue with him.

The conversation was cut short by the low rumble of Rush approaching in the truck. Marcie had opened her mouth to ask another question, but as soon as we both heard the engine and turned our heads to spy the sweep of headlights coming our way, whatever she'd been about to ask had been cut short.

I put my readers and the book away in my jacket pockets and stood up, setting my throw aside. I put my hands down to help Marcie to her feet, just as Rush pulled the truck to a stop behind us.

She put her hands in mine and they were icy cold, so I called out, "Hey, Rush! You got the heat on in there?"

"Yeah!" He heaved himself up and over the side of the bed and laid back against the back window of the truck's cab. "Have at, you can drop me off back at the house and take the truck if you want."

"Good man," I called lightly, opening up the passenger side of the truck for Marcie. She smiled and murmured her thanks and I realized just how tired she was. I shut her safely in the cab and asked as I walked around the back of the truck, "You want to pick some of this stuff up?"

"Nah, I'll get it tomorrow for you, D. Just put out the lantern."

I deviated and put out the lantern, and at least brought him his decanter of booze. He grinned, popped the top and took a swig straight from the bottle.

"Barbarian," I said with a grin and a chuckle.

"Back to reality," he said swallowing. "'Sides, I got you for a designated driver."

I laughed and opened up the driver's door, "That you do," I said. I got behind the wheel and put the automatic truck into gear and drove us back out to Bailey's house. I also made sure to hit as many ruts and potholes as I could on the way, Marcie laughing as Rush bounced around, cursing, in the back.

"Thanks a million, Rush!" I called as he hopped out of the bed back at the house.

"Almost made me spill my booze," he groused and I chuckled.

"Don't drink and ride," I told him, and he grinned and gave me the finger. Bailey came out onto the porch and waved. I blew my niece a kiss, like I did when she was just a little girl and a part of mine and Tilly's life, and she grinned and caught it, holding it to her heart.

"She was such a good kid," I said fondly as I turned the truck past my bike and toward the highway.

"She's a lovely young woman," Marcie said.

"Now that Rush has straightened her ass out some," I agreed. "Her mother is my late wife's sister."

"Ah, I was a little curious. I didn't see a family resemblance so much, so I figured that may have been the case."

"You're a clever lady, Marcie."

"Why, thank you, Dragon. You tend to use your head for somethin' other 'n a hat rack yourself."

I laughed and shook my head and we talked about my family some, about my boy Dray and adoptive daughter, Everett. I boasted a bit over my grandson and she practically gushed about her daughters and her grandbaby that was on the way.

Too soon, we were pullin' up at her back kitchen door, and the night was over. It'd been a good night. I had enjoyed myself, thoroughly, and I was glad she had, too. I walked her to her door and felt the urge to kiss her goodnight but I was a coward.

"That's strange," she said.

I frowned some, and asked, "What?"

"I don't have any roses blooming back here. You smell that?"

I smiled to myself. "I don't," I said. "Glad that you do, though."

She raised an eyebrow in the light of her back porch lamp and asked, "Why is that?"

"Oh," I said, backing away, "Gotta keep some things to myself, you know. Chicks dig a man of mystery."

She looked vaguely disappointed but laughed at what I said, "Fine. You keep your secrets, but do drive safe. I had a lovely evening."

"Will do, Marcie. You go on in now, and get warm."

She let herself into her house and I got back in the truck, the smell of roses overwhelming and, I felt like, a clear admonishment from my late wife. I could almost hear her, *Oh my God! Why didn't you kiss her? Do I have to take over your body?*

I laughed to myself, turned the truck around and headed back to pick up my bike from Bailey and Rush's place. The smell of roses became choking. I shook my head and turned my ass *back* around and pulled right up to Marcie's back door. She opened it up, her expression curious as I came around the truck.

I marched my ass right up the back steps and pulled her to me, covering her mouth with mine.

She made a wordless exclamation against my mouth, but didn't push away. While she'd stiffened up at first, it was a beautiful thing when she melted against me and returned the kiss.

I broke it and she swayed on her feet.

"See you soon, sugar."

"Okay," she said, breathlessly. "You promise?"

"I promise," I told her.

When I got back into the truck, the smell of roses had settled down some, and I smiled to myself.

"Don't be so damn smug," I muttered, and finally, I was on my way back to my second love in life. My bike.

10

M arcie…

"What're you doin' weekend after next?" he asked, his voice like velvet in my ear.

I cradled my phone between my neck and shoulder and smiled, saying, "Well, I don't know. Sounds like you've got somethin' in mind."

"I do. You think you can get off work?"

"I'll have to ask, you know the boss is one hard-assed bitch."

He laughed at that one and said, "Maybe I could butter her up for you."

"I think that could be arranged." I let my voice drop a little lower, and turned my back on my salon's front door. I was in here by myself. Don't ask me why I was so self-conscious.

"Well, all right then. Put her on the line."

"One moment, please…" I paused for dramatic effect and said, "Hello?"

He laughed and said, "That was awfully close to a dad joke."

"My ex was full of 'em with the girls. He may not have been a good husband all of the time, but he was and always has been a good daddy and a halfway-decent friend."

"I know I married my best friend," he said, and the edge of sad nostalgia was back in his voice. I could tell, this here was important. Us talkin' about our pasts and keepin' everything out in the open. It'd been nearly a week since I'd seen him last and I swear my lips still tingled from that kiss. I felt giddy and like a teenager every time we talked, which was every day, and yet, while both of us seemed excited about this connection, whatever it was… both of us remained cautious. I liked that. Felt like it was serious. Like it was real.

"I thought that was what you were supposed to do," I said. "Turns out, sometimes your best friend ain't necessarily meant for somethin' more. Speaking of which, Bobby's supposed to be here any minute to fix my sink."

"Good deal," he said, carefully. "What's wrong with the sink?"

"It's a salon. Even with hair traps the conditioner and crap likes to back them up after a while. He's comin' to snake the drain."

"Didn't know he was a plumber."

I laughed, "He's not, he's a river-boat pilot, but that doesn't keep him from being handy."

"I'll admit, I got mechanical expertise. Your car breaks down, I can sure fix it, but when it comes to indoor stuff like plumbing, I'd have to send one of the guys your way. They'd do it, too. That's part of what being club, being brothers, is all about. We help each other with things like that, no questions asked. When you're club, you're family."

"Sounds like club treats folks better 'n most families," I murmured and had to sigh.

I had a girl come in whose family was just awful to her. She was a grown adult and was still expected to do what they said and everything for them, and was just generally treated so poorly when she didn't. It'd like to break your heart. Family wasn't supposed to treat you that way; ike they're your family, but only when you were doin' what they wanted you to do for 'em.

She'd just left my salon not too long ago and though I didn't share her name, I shared the story.

Dragon grunted on the other end of the line.

"Sounds about right. Citizens just don't know how to treat each other for the most part anymore. It's one of the reasons we ain't typically got a use for 'em."

"Well, now!"

"You know that don't mean you," he declared.

And what about my daughters? Their families... I wondered, but I didn't say anything. I knew he hadn't meant anything by it, but it stung just the same.

I was saved by the bell. Literally, when the little brass bell above my salon door went off. I jumped slightly and turned around, a hand pressed to my chest as Bobby silently laughed at me.

"I've got to go, that would be Bobby," I said and Dragon made a 'uh-huh' noise.

"Call me later?" he asked.

"Of course!"

"And think about that weekend away."

"I surely will."

"All right, bye for now."

I smiled, warmed by his affectionate tone. "Bye for now," I echoed and lowered the phone from my ear.

"That the new boyfriend?" Bobby asked.

"Now that ain't none of your business, Bobby Lanham. How are yah?" I asked, setting my phone aside.

"Better 'n you," he said, with a twinkle in his eye. "Y'know, it works much better in yer favor, if you're facin' the door."

"Ohhh!" I waved him off, laughing, and he laughed, too.

"I got you good there, though. Hoo-boy!"

"Like t' scare the shit out of me," I agreed.

"Which sink is givin' you problems?" he asked, and pushed back through the swinging door.

I gave a gusty sigh and said, "The hair sink."

"Been a while since I had to come out and fix it," he said.

"That it has," I agreed. "I have a hair-trap, so I'm not sure what's goin' on with it."

I followed him back into the salon and sat down in my chair, swiveling it so I could face him. He set down his tool box next to the sink and started workin' on it.

"Well, y'know you gotta have at least a few years of buildup goin' on in here, unless you had someone else out since the last time I fixed it for you."

"Nope, you're my number one guy to call for the dirty jobs."

He chuckled. "Can't say I didn't earn that title," he said. "How come y' didn't have your new guy come out and have a look?"

"One, I don't have a new guy, and two, I do believe I just got done sayin' *that ain't none of your business.*"

He let out an exasperated sigh and said, "You may have left my ass, and for good reason!" He put up his hand to stave off my argument. "But I still love yah, Marcie, and you're still the mother of my children, so I gotta say, when Devon told me you were takin' up with that fella, I have some concerns."

I rolled my eyes. "I am a grown-ass woman, perfectly capable of makin' my own decisions and handling my own self. As you well remember." I know, I know, adding that last bit was a low blow but why everyone thought they had a right to tell me my business was beyond me!

"Well," he said weakly, "I'll have to give you that. The girls are just worried, is all."

"The girls, or Devon?" I asked.

"Well, Devon... Dylan did tell me you'd say to mind my own business."

"Which I've done twice now, don't make it a third," I warned sharply.

"Well then, who y' gonna get to fix yer sink?" he asked, hands on his hips.

I smirked.

"I'd figure it out," I said.

He shook his head and let out another loud breath. I knew what was comin' next and sure enough...

"Woman, you like to be the death of me," he said.

I smiled, "I know it." But I kept the bitter creeping thought that followed to myself, *Y' already killed me... broke my heart... maybe it's time to try something new. Maybe it's finally my turn to be happy.*

Which made me realize, Dragon and the time I got to spend with him? I can't remember the last time I smiled so much. Did that mean I was ready for a whole weekend away? Well, it was in two weeks, and I was likely to spend even more time with him between now and then.

Oh! Who was I kidding? I'd already made up my mind. Wasn't no sense in toyin' with the man! That wasn't something I wanted to do, not with him being so upfront and honest with me.

I would tell him yes, just as soon as the next time I talked to him.

11

Dragon...

    "You doin' alright?" I asked and dropped into a chair near Doc's. He looked up over his half-moon specs and gave me a lopsided grin.

"Doin' just fine, how about you?" he asked.

"To be honest," I said, "I don't rightly know."

"Oh?" He lowered his newspaper and frowned.

"Don't look at me that way, friend. It ain't my health or nothin' like that."

"The woman you was tryin' to fix me up with some weeks back?" he asked.

"Now, don't go puttin' it that way," I said.

He chuckled, "She under yer skin?"

"No!" I shifted a bit uncomfortably in my seat and Doc raised an eyebrow. "All right, maybe," I grudgingly admitted.

"So, what's the problem?" he asked.

"You think the club'll be able to accept me seein' the woman who hit Cell?" I asked.

"The club?" he asked back. "Or Blue and Hayley?"

"You know how that goes," I muttered.

"I hear you, but I think fer as smart as you are, yer bein' stupid."

I scowled. "How so?"

"You're worried about Blue and Hayley, you should really be talkin' to Blue and Hayley. Not me."

"Well, you got that right. I may have done somethin' a little impulsive…" I let the thought trail and he looked me over.

"What, I gotta drag it outta you?" he asked.

"I invited Marcie to ride with me on the Spring Lake Run."

His eyebrows shot up.

"My friend, you have an extraordinary grasp on your surroundings and ability for understanding people," he said. "Now, that being said, I don't think you even realize it. It has been my observation that a lot of the things you attribute to bein' your gut, or a bad or good feeling about this or that? Well, that ain't the case at all. You have a keen mind, one that works overtime in the front and the back. A lot of things you take for granted as bein' instinct, ain't. Your subconscious has just worked it all out before your front brain had the chance."

"Just what the devil are you getting at?" I asked, and was tryin' hard not to laugh.

"What I'm gettin' at, is if you didn't think any of us would be all right with you bringin' this woman around us, you wouldn't have invited her. You would have gone to the folks in your club and made certain, if you felt somethin' would be off about it."

I nodded slowly, absorbing what it was he was tellin' me and I couldn't deny he was right.

"You got a point, there, Doc."

"I know I do, so if you're havin' second thoughts after you've already asked her, it has more to do with *you* than anyone else and how they might take it." He shook his head. "Besides, she could be a purple-people-eater from fuckin' Mars or some shit – none of the rest of us would care."

"Why's that?" I demanded.

"On account of whatever she is to you, she's makin' you happier 'n we've seen you in a minute… and by 'minute', I mean 'since Tilly died'. Somethin' about you is just…" he searched my face. "lighter, somehow. Like you're not carryin' as much. It's good."

"That's just my fuckin' haircut," I grumbled and he laughed.

"Which, if I recall, we have courtesy of Ms. Marcie What's-her-last-name."

I chuckled. "So you're tellin' me I should have a chat with Blue and Hayley about it if I feel weird and stop bein' such a damn knucklehead."

"If the first makes you feel better, then yeah. Definitely the second, though."

I shook my head and heaved myself to my feet.

"Where y' goin'?"

"Dinner."

"At a certain greasy spoon diner?"

"How'd you guess?"

He shook out his paper and went back to readin' it. Didn't even bother to answer.

I chuckled again to myself and went and found my jacket and cut. My helmet was with my bike. I did that here at the club, but not out and about. Learned that lesson the hard way one night, leavin' it with my bike when I was just a kid.

I'd gone into one of them mini-mart places for a pack of smokes and some road beers. There was this drunk motherfucker at the counter and I guess they wouldn't let him use the bathroom on account of he wasn't a payin' customer or somethin'. He goes storming out into the lot and I bought my shit, only to come out of the place to see this guy droppin' a deuce in my fuckin' helmet, which was hangin' off my handlebar.

It was funny now, but then? I'd flown into a temper and beat the brakes off the guy 'til he was nothin' but a broken, bleeding, sobbing pile.

I'd seen the same kind of anger in my boy after his momma died, and I didn't know how to fix it for him. Didn't know how to straighten him out. Me? I'd learned the hard way.

The first and only time I'd caught Tilly in the mouth with the back of my hand, she'd kicked me right in the balls and I'd gone down like a ton of bricks.

She'd walked out on me right then and there. Only took me back by the grace of whatever God there was and on the promise I'd get that part of me under control. That woman did more to rein my temper in than anything.

I'd been hoping Dray would find the same, but it turned out to be Trig and his woman to teach him that particular lesson, far before he ever fucked up as hard as I did. He still did find a woman just like his mother, though. Everett wasn't about to take any of that boy's shit, and I was happy for him.

I don't think most men realized the benefit of havin' a strong, smart, and calculating queen by his side to rule with him over his personal kingdom. Any man who thought he had it right all of the time clearly didn't. Any man arrogant enough to walk down the street naked, without the benefit of one of his own to cry out the emperor had no clothes, was a man that was doomed to ultimate failure.

I'd been lucky. Then I got arrogant. It was an arrogance I couldn't afford, thinkin' I was slicker than owl shit and that nothin' could or would stick. Maybe it didn't in a legal sense, but the universe schooled me the hardest way it could, and my poor wife had been the one to lose her life in the lesson.

There was a saying that went something like 'It's never too late to change your ways' and while it was true? Well, it wasn't too late for me. Just too late for her. I swore never again.

Never say never, lover...

Her voice caressed the inside of my skull and I chuckled.

"Never again am I gonna let someone else pay for my sins, baby. But you're right. I did swear I'd never love again, but I damn sure feel somethin' for that firecracker. I'd ask you what you think, but you already know I know."

I listened, breathing slow and deep, waiting for something, anything, else from my late wife, but of course, there was nothing. Well, nothing except that familiar fractured ache in the center of my chest. But I'd be lying if I didn't say it'd diminished by far from what it'd been.

I rode out to the diner that Hayley's father owned and she waitressed at. The place was the center of Hayley's world, and as such, it'd become the center of Blue's. I could find him there when he wasn't working road crew, and sure enough, when I went through the door, he was off to the side doctoring up some coffee, Hayley behind the counter returning the pot to the warmer.

"Hey, D." Blue called out. I smiled and went over to his booth and slid into it, across the table from him.

"Hey, Blue."

"What brings you in here?"

"Was hoping to talk to you and Hayley."

Blue gave me a charmed sort of smile, had it been on anyone else I would have called it sweet, but you don't say a badass biker smiled sweetly at you. Except maybe Reaver, but that fucker was crazy anyhow.

"This about the woman you've been seeing over the last few weeks? The one that was involved in Cell's accident?"

I hitched in a bit of a laugh and took it back. These bikers gossiped more 'n a bunch of little old ladies at Marcie's salon.

"That would be the one," I agreed. It hadn't gone unnoticed by me, or any of the rest of the boys, that after Cell had died, Blue had somehow managed to find his voice. Gone was the silence, but when it was a big group of us, he still maintained a shy silence.

Hayley came over and slid into the booth beside her man, covering his hand with hers and said, "I heard you say you wanted to talk to the both of us. I only have a minute, but what can we help you with, Dragon?"

Blue smiled and looked her over with adoration. "I believe he's here looking for permission of sorts."

"Oh?" Hayley looked me over, smiling. "So, things are going well with the woman that Cell hit? How is she?"

Interesting phrasing, 'the woman that Cell hit'. It wasn't untrue, but good luck getting Marcie to see it that way.

"I asked her to join me for the Lake Run, but I wanted to talk to you two and make sure you were all right with it. If yer not, I have no trouble rescinding the invitation. I feel like I probably shoulda asked you first, but at the same time, I felt like you'd be all right with it."

"Of course we are," Blue said, and he and Hayley exchanged a look.

"It wasn't her fault," Hayley said. "Cell rode like a maniac. It scared the hell out of me, getting on the back of his motorcycle. It was an accident, and if it was anyone's fault, it was his. I'm not mad about it anymore. It hurts, sure, but the blame rests with Cell. She was making her legal turn. He was being an idiot. That's pretty much the end of the story."

I sighed, "I wish it were as simple as that."

Hayley's face crumbled. "Oh, no… is she blaming herself? That poor thing! Yes. Bring her. I would like to meet her." She got up smoothly and without further ado asked, "What can I get you?"

I smiled and loved that girl in that moment for her selflessness and generosity. I ordered the diner's pot roast and she smiled and asked, "Extra gravy?"

"On the meat and potatoes," I agreed. "You'd like to think I've eaten here before."

She winked at me. "Not nearly enough." And with that, she walked away.

I turned back to Blue, who was watching me, smiling softly. He shook his head.

"You know us, Dragon. You also know, that if he'd lived Cell probably would have broken or destroyed us by now." He looked sad for a moment. "And I likely wouldn't have been strong enough to stop it."

"Don't talk like that, Blue. You know we would have had your back," I said.

"Oh, I know. You guys have been amazing," he said. "But I don't know how amazing I would have been if it'd come to it."

"You got some strong women in your corner, Blue. I'm not just talkin' about Hayley, either. You think Dani would have let you fall that far? Or that she'd let Thirteen sit on his ass?"

Blue smiled and swallowed hard. "I don't feel like I do near enough for you all as you do for us," he said.

"How about your boy?" I asked.

"No signs," he said. "Not yet." But he looked troubled.

"There ain't gonna be, either." I said with false confidence.

We'd met Cell's parents, his sister, at the funeral. They'd come, and they'd been grateful that we'd taken care of everything. They hadn't known what to do. They'd talked quietly with Blue and Hayley, and from what I'd gathered, they were good, God-fearing citizens. The kind of innocent people who worked hard all their lives and did every-thing they could for their kids. Cell hadn't been abused, far from it. He'd been loved, cared for; he'd just been the epitome of 'the bad seed.' Born evil, through and through, a true sociopath. Serial-killer material.

His sister was downright grateful he was dead. I saw the haunted expression on her face and in her eyes. I'd bet even money he'd killed her pets, maybe even tried to kill her, when they were growing up. To say that his family wasn't sorry he was gone was an understatement. If anything, their expressions spelled relief, guilt, and a deep sorrow. The sorrow, not because he was gone, but because they were glad for it, and no one should feel glad for the death of their kin.

I didn't subscribe to the same philosophy, though. It was one of the things that marked me as 'other' from polite society. Someone done you enough wrong, blood or not, they weren't family no more. You had every right to feel the way you felt about them dying. I know I was glad for a few kin's passing. I loved my momma, but my daddy could burn in hell, the drunk abusive fuck.

I turned out just like him, I just channeled my ruthlessness into protecting what was mine, rather than destroying it. I'd be a liar to myself and the world if I tried to deny our similarities. I was a chip off the ol' block. I was glad fer the fact I'd managed to break the cycle when it came to Tilly, when it came to Dray. Honestly, though. I think she had more to do with it than I did, my guiding light out of that particular darkness.

"Only time will tell," Blue murmured and I smiled.

"You just keep loving that boy as if he were your own and everything is going to come out okay," I said.

Blue gave me a blank look and said, "He is my own."

I smiled and nodded. "You're a good man, Blue. One of our best. I'm proud to have you in this chapter. I'm happy to be of any assistance you might need. All of us are. You're home, and what's done is done and in the past. For all of us. It's time to look to the future."

Blue smiled and said, "We're all perfectly happy in our present with a future that's bright. It's your turn."

I grinned and nodded. "I reckon you might be right."

"So, when do you see her again?" he asked.

"I don't know. I'm hoping this week, but I'm not sure what to go do this time. I kinda pulled out all the stops last time."

He grinned. "You know, Hayley was sayin' there's a farmer's market the next county over she wanted to check out."

"You thinkin' an accidental meetup might be in order?"

"I'm thinking it would be a good idea to lay old ghosts to rest before you brought her on something like a Lake Run."

"You got a very valid point there, Blue."

He laughed. "Shut up. You already thought of it. That's part of why you're here."

I chuckled and nodded some. "True, true, I just didn't know how I was gonna ease her into it. A meeting with you two."

His face sobered and he sighed. "Are you sure this is the best way?"

"I think that it would be the easiest on her, yes. Though I don't much like the sneakiness of it."

Blue seemed relieved by my take on it and I couldn't say I blamed him. The one thing about Cell was, *everything* was a manipulation. He'd been with the man longest, loving even when he couldn't be loved in return. That was one hell of a mark left behind on his soul.

He finally nodded. "I'll see if I can find a sitter. Hayley and I need some time alone together anyways. It's been a while since we took an afternoon for ourselves."

"You know we're all here to help."

"I know, but until we know, I'm just afraid to have Damon around the other kids. You know, just in case."

"Blue, he ain't big enough or strong enough to be a problem."

"I know, but what if he bites another kid or something?" he asked, shifting uncomfortably.

I laughed. "Dray was a biter," I said, and he raised his eyebrows. "Kids bite, doesn't mean he's like Cell. I know you both are scared, but you gotta let him be a kid, too. You can't act like the world needs protecting from him. I know it's hard, but Damon can pick up on things like that, so do other people. You treat him like there's something wrong with him, other people will start thinkin' there is, then he'll start thinkin' it, and it'll be downhill from there."

"Shit, you're right. I feel like we're walking a tightrope, D."

"Maybe y'are, but you're forgettin' something."

"What's that?" he asked curiously.

I winked at him. "The safety net that is your club and your brothers underneath you and your little family of three."

He sat back and looked slightly gobsmacked and I smiled bigger. "You just let that finish sinkin' in. "

12

Marcie...

"So, where we going?" I asked him, when he showed up on Sunday morning.

"I figured it'd be nice to head on over to this farmer's market the next county over. They got all kinds of things, someone said it'd be a good time."

"You know, that sounds real nice. What if we want to buy some groceries, though?" I leaned a hip against the porch rail and crossed my arms.

"That's what the saddlebags are cleared out for. Plus, I got a couple of backpacks. Just try not to go too crazy."

He grinned and I came down the steps and crunched across the gravel of my yard.

"Baby, 'Crazy' is my middle name, I thought you knew that."

He laughed and leaned over the back of the bike. I couldn't help but smile, and met him halfway. We kissed, and it was nice. Comfortable and easy, with that glimmer of excitement.

"I have to be back in time for Sunday dinner. About three o'clock, if at all possible, so I can cook."

"I'll have you back in time," he assured me. "What's on the menu?"

"I hadn't really thought about it, none. I took pork chops out to thaw, so I guess I'd better figure it out."

"Well, come on then, sugar. We're burnin' daylight."

He swung a leg over the back of his machine and I got on behind him.

The ride out to the farmer's market was a nice one. The sun was out, and some of the old roads and lanes we took were under a canopy of trees. The dappled light in combination with the wind was something fresh and uplifting to my spirits. I hadn't intended to have him for dinner, but the more I thought about it, the more I realized that I really liked Dragon. I was happy when I was with him, we had some things in common, and he was both an intelligent and thoughtful man.

I wanted to see where things went, but it also seemed a little impossible at the same time. I didn't know if my family would even give him a chance, and even though Rush had been kind, what about the rest of his club? How would the people closest to his man that I killed ever be able to accept me?

I didn't know. I did know one thing, though. He and I were both a little too old for any Romeo-and-Juliet type shenanigans. While I didn't want to hurt anyone else, I also wanted to be happy... which is why I had to ask myself, why the hell couldn't life ever be easy? Just once. Just for one damn minute.

We pulled up to the farm hosting the market. Rows of tents were set up under the sun in an open field. Another field of tamped-down and flattened yellow grass was used as a parking area. We followed the directions of some volunteers in yellow vests and parked in with a line of other motorcycles.

"Woah, here, let me have that," he said. I plucked the helmet I'd hung by the chinstrap back off the handlebar and handed it over to him. He locked one in each saddlebag.

"What's that about?" I asked, laughing, looking around at some of the other bikes, their helmets hanging off their handlebars.

"Ah, well..." He laughed and said, "Have I got a story for you! I was a kid, and I went into one of them mini-marts for a pack of smokes and some road beers..."

I couldn't believe it, over thirtysome-odd years ago, one crazy drunk and he *still* locked up his helmets to this day. I laughed. I laughed and laughed and laughed, as we walked over the dusty grass to the farmer's market entrance.

"Oh, my god! That's so disgusting! It's not funny, I shouldn't be laughing."

"You kiddin' me? It's hilarious, and you should absolutely be laughin'."

I laughed all over again and asked, "So what'd you do?"

"Eh... I lost my temper," he said, and had the grace to look embarrassed. "I beat the brakes off that dude. Not one of my prouder moments."

"Oh, well... you were young," I declared. "I'm sure you've matured some since then."

"I'd like to think so," he said. "At least in all the ways that really matter." He bounced his eyebrows and knocked his shoulder gently into mine. I laughed and wrapped my arms loosely around his one as we walked. I all but felt aglow when he twined his fingers between mine, holding my hand loosely in his own.

The market was beautiful and full of good things. I bought some gorgeous heirloom tomatoes for sliced tomatoes and a whole bunch of green beans to put with onions and bacon. I found some good-lookin' red potatoes and bought those, too. I even bought two of the market's canvas totes to carry it all in.

With dinner for tonight settled, I cast an eye towards shopping for the rest of the week, moving with Dragon from stall to stall, stopping to smell the fresh-cut flowers.

"Hey, D!"

Dragon and I turned as one toward the call and I bit my lower lip. The man was tall and thin, but it was that kind of lean musculature that a lot of my romance authors described as 'whipcord over bone'. The woman beside him had her long dark hair swept up into a hair clip at the back, a sweep of bangs over her forehead. Her lovely dark eyes looked me over as they approached.

"Hey, Blue!"

Blue... Blue... the name tickled my memory but I couldn't quite place it, yet.

Then I realized with a jolt who they were.

Blue and Hayley, the two people that loved the man you killed.

All the hair stood up on the back of my neck, goosebumps marching down my arms as I stared at them. A tingle overtook me and I could feel the blood drain from my face. I stood stock-still and tried not to sway on my feet as they stopped in front of us.

"Marcie," Dragon said gently, "I'd like for you to meet my man Blue and his Ol' Lady, Hayley."

I swallowed hard, tears starting in my eyes as I tried to get my mouth to work.

"Oh, don't do that," the girl said, sympathetically.

Her, sympathetic to me… I lost it, then, my face crumbling, an ugly cry coming on – and she reached out without hesitation and hugged me. Me, who'd killed someone she loved dearly.

Lord, I thought. *Lord, I don't deserve their forgiveness.* Seems that he and they saw fit to give it to me anyway.

13

D ragon...

    I think the talk with Hayley and Blue went well. Marcie seemed alright, although our shopping trip was pretty much done after that. We went back to the bike, her hand wrapped in a death grip around my own as she worked through her emotions. The ride back to her place was a silent one, and I could tell she was lost inside her own head. Still, I think the wind therapy did her some good. She was much calmer by the time I shut off the bike out back of her little house. She got off and handed me over her helmet, which I sat on the seat while I got into the saddlebags for her groceries.

"Runnin' into them like that was no happy accident, was it?" she asked, finally.

I handed her one of the canvas bags full of vegetables.

"No," I said simply.

"That's your one 'Get out of jail free' card, Dragon. And I mean it," she said coldly.

I stood and faced her over the back of my bike.

"Now my intentions were good, Marcie –"

"I don't care!" She cut me off. "I spent a good part of my marriage lettin' myself be manipulated and I swore never again. Now, I mean it! You either be up-front and honest with me from here on out, or you can kick rocks, mister!"

I searched her oh-so-serious face, her blue eyes shuttered and hurt, and I nodded.

"You're right. Good intentions or not, I can see I hurt your feelin's. I'm sorry for that. That I did not intend. I just wanted to show you that none of us hold any ill will towards you." I thought about it and amended, "Except maybe Archer. That grouchy bastard can hold a grudge from here to kingdom come, but even he comes around eventually."

She held still and I could see a war of emotion in her eyes. A longing to believe me, but at the same time, I'd hurt her. Damaged her trust… I should have seen that coming.

I went around the bike, sighing, and took it as encouraging that she didn't back away. I pulled her into my arms and held her close for a minute and after a while, she relaxed, and hugged me back.

"I'm sorry," I murmured next to her ear. "I really just wanted to fix it, before we went too deep."

She sniffed and said, "Well, turnabout *is* fair play, boy. You might as well stay for dinner and meet the family. You can help by cleaning these beans for me.

I chuckled. I was made of sterner stuff, didn't much care if her family liked me or not. It wasn't gonna make me go away. I'd decided I liked Marcie, and I wanted to stick around. It pretty much took an act of God to sway me once I made up my mind like that.

I pulled back and she sniffed again, dashing a knuckle under each eye and asking, "You smell roses?"

I shook my head, smiling to myself.

"Nope."

I do believe my late wife had spoken, and the verdict was, she liked Marcie, too.

I got the rest of her groceries out of the other saddlebag and put our helmets inside before lockin' 'em up securely again. I followed her up the back steps to her kitchen door, paused to wipe my feet on the mat, and followed her inside.

"You can hang your jacket on the back of one of the chairs there, or I can put it in the closet. Up to you," she said.

"If you don't mind," I said. "I'd like to keep my colors in sight."

She smiled and nodded simply.

"I won't pretend to understand the why of it, but I'd right like to learn," she said.

"I appreciate that," I said, dropping the heavy leather over the back of the chair.

"Beans," she said sternly, dropping the plastic bag full of 'em on the counter and setting two bowls down next to 'em.

"Yes, Ma'am." I saluted and went for them. "You don't mind, I'm going to step out for a smoke."

"Fine," she said. "But take 'em with you."

I smiled and she smiled back, and I headed out to the porch. I could tell she was getting over her mad. I was definitely gonna have to adjust my ways with this firecracker of a woman, but that was all right. Nothin' worth havin' was ever easy. Life in general had taught me that.

She came out with another bowl full of red potatoes and a strainer and sat up on the step behind me. She'd put on an apron and she pulled a paring knife from the pocket and started peeling potatoes from the bowl, droppin' the finished spuds into the strainer and leavin' the peels in the bowl they come from.

"Do me a favor and put your bean leavings in here with these peels. Makes for good compost for my garden."

"Sure thing," I murmured. I took a drag off my cigarette and blew the smoke away from us.

She chuckled and asked me, "You ever consider quittin' them things?"

"Not really," I said. "Why, they a turn-off?"

"I'd be lyin' if I said no," she said.

I nodded. "Never had much reason to."

"How about a long life and to see your grandbaby grow to be a man?" she asked,

I chuckled and said, "You might have a point there. I'm just about the only smoker left out of the rest of my men."

I glanced up behind me, and had a moment to myself to take in how beautiful she was, a slight smile on her lips, blue eyes focused on her finely-weathered hands as she carefully pared the skin off the potato in 'em. She was a natural beauty. Didn't wear no makeup. Didn't need none of it, either.

"Anyone ever tell you you're a beautiful woman?" I asked, and her hands stilled. Her eyes flicked to mine and I could see the answer in them before she even spoke it.

"Not for a real long time, and usually just after they found themselves in trouble with me."

I smiled to myself and said, "Well then, remind me to tell you when I'm not in trouble with you."

She laughed and nudged me with her denim-clad knee and went back to peeling her potato.

"You like collard greens?" she asked.

"I surely do," I said. "Been a while since I had any done right."

"Got a big batch that's gettin' to be on their last legs in the 'fridgerator. I best do 'em up for tonight or I'm gonna lose 'em. I hate wastin' food."

"Don't they take hours and hours on the stove?" I asked.

"Oh, honey. That's what a pressure cooker is for. I like mine so much I went out and bought another one just like it. Best way t' make greens and mashed patatuhs." I smiled hard at how she pronounced 'potatoes'. It was such a southern thing, and a strange sort of peaceful comfort, hearin' her say it the way she did.

"I have t' confess, I ain't much in the kitchen. Most of the time, I finish cookin', one of the boys asks me what it is and I have to tell 'em, 'Well, I don't know, but it's hot, it's brown, and there's a lot of it.'"

She about died laughing, patted me on the shoulder and got up, tears at the corners of her eyes and said, "Best leave the cookin' to me, then." She trailed into the house muttering, "Hot, brown and a lot of it... God love him."

I smiled and kept snappin' beans, droppin' the discarded ends into the bowl of potato leavin's. I finished my cigarette, and took everything back in the house after I aired out some.

I asked her, "Where you want this when I'm done?" and indicated the bowl of scraps.

"There's one of them big gray bins out by the shed back there. I dump 'em in there and turn it with the shovel leanin' up next to it."

"Good to know. I'm almost done with these."

"Thank you," she said, and gave me another smile.

"This calm and peace we got between us, does that mean I'm forgiven?"

She looked over from where she rinsed her potatoes at the sink and nodded carefully.

"People aren't perfect," she said. "Your heart was in the right place, and you were right, it needed to happen. Meetin' 'em, clearing the air, whatever it is you wanna call it. Just, like I said, please be honest with me. If you'd told me, I wouldn't have *wanted* to go, but I would have."

"That was my thought," I said honestly. "I really was just tryin' to spare you some dread."

She smiled and nodded gracefully and said, "And how are you doin' over there?"

"Me? Oh, I'm just peachy. Why you ask?"

"Well, yer meetin' my girls for the first time ever. They should be around any minute."

I nodded, "I'm used to people hatin' on me, sweetheart. I knew the life I was choosin' when I chose it. It'd be nice if they liked me, but I don't expect it none."

"Well," she said, sounding dismayed. "I hope they learn to like you, too. Otherwise we might be in for a load of uncomfortable Thanksgivin' holidays."

I chuckled and finished up the beans, standin' and bringin' 'em over. She took the bowl and said to me, "Under the sink," when I held up the bag they'd come from.

"What can I do for you now?" I asked.

"Well, you can get into the pantry and get down one of my jars of applesauce for me."

I gave a nod and went in through the closet door she indicated. I was a little blown away by how organized it was and that a good ninety-percent of what she had on the shelves in here was stuff she'd obviously done up herself, each Mason jar carefully labeled with the contents.

"You want one of the quart jars or a pint?" I called back.

"Grab me down a quart, would yah?"

"You got it." I brought down one of the big heavy jars and the back door opened up as I stepped out the closet, so-to-speak.

"Mamma – oh!"

The pretty blonde girl stopped cold just inside the door, eyes wide as she met mine. I smiled and gave a polite not of my head, figuring this one must be Dylan. She wasn't heavily pregnant, as Marcie had described her daughter Devon to be.

"You must be Dylan," I said, and she looked taken aback.

"You know my name?" she asked.

"Well, of course he knows your name, girl! What, you don't think I talk about you? Now what is it?" Marcie asked from where she turned one of her pressure cookers on, pressing this button and that.

"Oh, I tried to make your pie recipe." She held out an aluminum-foil-covered round pie plate, and made a face like someone killed her favorite dog.

"Oh, dear, what happened?" Marcie asked, taking the pie plate.

"It didn't turn out like yours!" The girl pouted and it was adorable. I had to laugh.

"Rarely does yer pie turn out the way momma makes it. Something about needing to be a mamma yourself," I offered helpfully.

"Piss on that!" Marcie cried. "Has nothin' to do with it."

I laughed, "Well, I tried."

"Hi, I *am* Dylan," her youngest said with a shy smile. She stuck out her hand and I took it, shaking it gently.

"Hi, Dylan. Folks call me Dragon."

She looked at me curiously and took back her hand and glanced around, her eyes falling on my colors hanging on the back of the chair. She swallowed nervously and I chuckled.

"'S'alright, I'm used to it."

Marcie looked up from where she'd taken a fork to the pie, chewing thoughtfully before she asked, "You use any nutmeg?"

Dylan, distracted from me for the moment, looked at her mother, aghast. "That wasn't on the recipe you give me!"

The two women fell into arguing over what looked like a perfectly good apple pie to me, when the back door opened again.

"Mamma, that motorcycle better not belong to…" Her oldest daughter froze just inside the door, her husband nearly crashing into her back as I gave a wave.

Well, this wasn't gonna be awkward at all… Marcie had it handled, though. A hand went to her hip and she stared her oldest down. Dylan ducked and ran for cover, going around her mamma and pulling down plates to set the table.

"Devon Arlyna Lanham, now I *know* you did *not* just come into my house tellin' me who I could and could not have in it as a guest. In front of said guest, no less!"

"Mamma – "

"Don't you 'Mamma' me, girl! I know I raised you better than that! Now you apologize to that man and introduce yourself proper, or you can leave." Martha looked past her older daughter to her son-in-law.

"Sorry about that, Richard."

"It's all good, Mamma Marcie," Richard choked out, trying not to laugh, and his laughter withered under the look his wife gave him.

"If y'all don't mind," I said, "I've really got to use the restroom. Uh, Marcie, where would that be?"

"Down the hall, second door on the left, sweetheart," Marcie said, still staring her eldest daughter and her husband down, her gaze still hard with warning. I could tell she was pissed and I was stayin' out of it.

"Wish I'd thought of that first," Dylan muttered out of the side of her mouth as I passed her and I chuckled.

By the time I got done doin' my business, washin' my hands with the nice little soaps Marcie had out, and dryin' 'em thoroughly on the matching little hand towel on the towel ring by the sink, her sharp words had settled some and it'd gone quiet in the kitchen. I waited a few heartbeats extra, just to be sure all was well, before I went back out.

Rich, the son-in-law, was in the living room in one of the two wing-back chairs, facin' the television over the fireplace. He had his feet up and looked up when I passed by the archway from the living room to the kitchen. He gave me a nod, his expression curious, and I could see some of them law-enforcement wheels turnin' in his head.

I smiled to myself and went over by Marcie and leaned my butt up against the counter while she melted some shortening in a cast iron skillet. Her girls eyed us warily from the dining room where they set the table.

"Everythin' alright?" I asked, low.

Marcie forced a smile around her simmering anger and said, "Peachy keen, why don't you and Rich find somethin' to watch on TV?"

"Well, that's a 'get the hell out my kitchen' if I ever heard one."

She wrinkled her nose cutely and grinned impishly, and I chuckled and did as the woman asked. Her oldest put her hands on my colors as if to move 'em and I froze.

"If'n you don't mind, them there are somethin' sacred to the likes of us... no pun intended. You'd like 'em moved, I'm happy to move 'em for you, but in our culture the only one to touch 'em should be me, one of my brothers, or my ol' lady." I tried to keep my tone gentle. I didn't want her to feel like I was snappin' at her.

She took her hands away and said, "I'm sorry, I didn't know."

"It's all good, darlin'. I know you didn't. Would you like me to move 'em?"

"Yes, please."

"That I can do." I went over and picked up my jacket and cut and draped them over my arm. I took them into the living room with me and laid 'em over the arm of the couch, before taking the other wing-back chair facing the television.

"You a big sports guy, Mr. Dragon?" Rich asked.

"Can't say that I am," I said.

"Oh, yeah? What do you like to watch?"

"The science channel, history channel, mostly."

"No shit?" he asked, surprised. "You into those war documentaries?"

"Sometimes. Been watching a lot about the Vikings lately."

"You like that show, *Vikings*?"

"Y'know, I didn't think I would, but I caught an episode when it first started up back when and I really did enjoy it..."

Turns out, Rich and I had some real genuine interest in some of the same shows. The common ground helped some, and was a good way to break the ice. Maybe this whole 'meetin' the family' thing wasn't gonna be as disastrous as I'd thought it might be.

14

M arcie...

"All I'm sayin' is it's not real fair. I gotta do somethin'," I told him. He laughed at me and I smiled real big.

We were supposed to be leavin' in the mornin' for this weekend away he had planned and he'd come clean and told me it was their annual Spring Lake Run, whatever that was. I'd had questions, and he'd patiently answered every one of 'em for me, late into last night. I'd spent all day today baking up a bunch of my apple pies special.

"Sugar, we can't take a bunch of pies on the bike," he said kindly.

"I know that! Don't be silly. You said there was a repair truck and cars with the kids, didn't you?"

"I do believe I did."

"Well, all right, then. I'll pack these up in my car and bring 'em over in the mornin'. No need to pick me up."

He laughed again and said, "Okay, all right. You know how to get here?"

"No, but my phone does. Just text me the address!"

"How 'bout comin' tonight?" he asked.

"Well, why not? I've already got a bag packed, and these pies'll keep, if you got a 'fridgerator there."

"Oh, we got fridges. You, uh, wanna stay the night, maybe?"

I smiled and said, "You bet your ass, I do."

"Well then, come on down, Ms. Marcie."

"I'll see you soon."

"All right then, just do me a favor. If you're gonna be gone for days at a time, lock yer damn door."

I chuckled and said, "Yes, Daddy." I could *hear* him cringe on the other end of the line and it made me like to laugh my head off. I hung up before he could say anything else, excited to see him, and knowin' if he kept me on the phone I'd like to never get out of here.

I opened up the back of my car and ferried the eight pies I'd made, in the big ol' box I had 'em in, out there first. Then, I quickly threw what I'd planned on wearin' tomorrow into the top of my overnight bag and brought it out there. I did what he asked, locked up my kitchen door, and turned for the car.

"Dammit to hell!" I cursed. I put the overnight bag in the back and shut the door before going back into my house for my damn purse. I re-locked everything tight and got behind the wheel.

I got my phone to workin' and tellin' me where to go, put it up on the mount for it, and my excitement damn near bubbling over, got under-way, headed to where the lady in my phone told me to.

The driveway was steep, and right off the highway. I almost missed it. It had a spikey, almost imposing wrought iron fence around the whole property, but once I was up into the parking lot, things smoothed out and looked much more welcoming. Especially since Dragon was standing out front by the line of motorcycles, waitin' for me.

He sucked down a last drag off his cigarette and flicked it into the gravel and walked out to meet me. I stopped and he blew out the smoke before getting to my window, which glided down smoothly with the flick of a switch.

"Hi there," I said shyly. I had a hard time believin' someone as handsome as he was could be interested in me, but somehow, here we were.

"Hey, sugar." He gripped the edge of my window and put his head inside the car, pressing his mouth to mine. My eyes drifted shut and even though he tasted like tobacco smoke, I didn't care. I kissed him back and the stress of the day just sort of melted off of me. He smiled against my mouth, my lips curving to echo his and leaned back.

"Got anything you want me to take in?" he asked.

"Just the pies."

"Sure, gimme just a sec." He leaned back and let out a piercing whistle. A man came out the front door of the building, grinning, and stepped out from under the porch-like shingled awning over the door into the dying daylight .

"Sup, D?"

"Yeah, Reave, you mind takin' this box of pies in the club?"

"Sure thing, they up for grabs, or they for the Lake Run?"

"What the hell d'you think?" Dragon asked, laughing.

"Aww, dammit! I had to try. What's up, Marcie, how you doing?" he asked.

I smiled up into sparkling blue eyes like a huskie's and said, "Oh, I'm fine. How're you?"

"Good!" He went to the back of my car and I hit the button for the locks.

"Want the bag, too?" he called.

"I'll get that," Dragon said.

"Cool, see you inside."

Reaver hefted the big cardboard box and yelled "Somebody get the door, Marcie made us pie!"

I laughed and a big man with long blonde hair stepped out and held the door for Reaver who said, "Thanks, my man!"

"You good, D? Anything else?"

"All good, thanks, Trig."

"Ma'am," Trig gave me a nod. I smiled and gave him a little wave.

"Why don't you go on and pull up where there's space over there."

"You got it."

I pulled in where he indicated and shut off my car. He pulled my bag out of the back and closed the hatch while I got my phone and my purse and what-have-you all together.

I got out of the car and he backed me up against the side of it, his mouth finding mine once again.

"Well, I can tell you're happy to see me," I murmured, and he pressed himself against me fully. Oh my, he was *very* happy to see me.

"I think I may have missed you, Sugar."

I smiled and kissed him one more time.

"I missed you, too," I whispered into his mouth.

"Mm, let's get inside, get the meet 'n greet over with, so I can have you to m'self."

"I like the sound of that," I said softly.

"I suspected you might," he replied with a slow, sexy grin and a wink.

We went to the door hand-in-hand and it opened up before we got to it, the big blond man holding it for us as we slipped past his large frame into the dimly-lit interior of what looked like a bar.

I looked around carefully, smiling half-charmed. It was nice in here. Clearly, Dragon and his men had spent time and care in putting this place together. From the polished bartop, to the bottles lined up in front of a stained glass window with the club's logo done in bits of mosaic glass adhered together by some magic and backlit with a warm light.

The furniture had been made sturdy, the tables and chairs having the same touch to them as the outdoor loungers we'd sat in on Dragon's niece's racehorse farm. Dragon glowed with pride at the expression on my face as I took it all in.

"Y'all have done real nice in here," I said admiringly.

"It was a work--in-progress for the longest time, but yeah. It finally came together," the big blond man said. He smiled and held out a hand. "I'm Trigger."

"Pleasure to meet you, Trigger."

"That there is my ol' lady, Sunshine."

A soft voice from behind the bar said, "Hi."

I turned around to see her, another woman, and Reaver come out of the doorway leading back to what looked like an industrial kitchen.

"I'm Reaver, and this is my Doll," he said.

"Hi." The other woman curled her fingers in a wave, her dark hair brushing her shoulders in what was clearly an in-between phase of growing it out. I smiled at her warmly and said, "Hello. I'm Marcie."

"Pleasure to finally meet you, Marcie," Sunshine said.

Dragon gently took my elbow and said, "If y'all don't mind, I'm going to take Marcie back and get her settled in for tonight."

"No, go ahead."

"Not at all," the responses came.

I blushed and said, "I guess we'll see y'all later."

Chuckles and giggles chorused, and Dragon pointed past a bay of curtained windows, past the end of the bar on the opposite side, to a cavernous hall beyond. I went the way he indicated, curious as to what was behind the curtains inside those windows.

I didn't ask, I figured if I was meant to, I'd find out. There was a sort of hub just past that fishbowl, several doors set in the walls around us, most marked 'Restroom', and two halls, one leading off to the left and one leading straight back. He stopped and pointed to the doors.

"Bathroom and bathroom. That there," he indicated a pair of lovely double doors, "leads into the media room. Got a bunch of seating, movies, and a big screen TV." He indicated the hall leading straight back and said, "That there leads out back to the fire-pit, the door on the left is Doc's room, the one on the right is storage. My room is down this way." He led me down the hall to the left where there was another bank of windows off to the right, the curtains in here drawn back, a big table that also had to be Rush's work inside.

"Just finished this part. There were some more club rooms for members along here. They moved to the outbuilding we finished out back to make way for a more secure chapel so we could hold church while the girls and the kids moved around. My room's right here, the opposite side. Here we go." He opened a door and switched on a light.

"Did some cleanin' up," he said. "Didn't think you'd be about that bachelor life."

"Oh!" I waved him off. "Seems like Rush has been a busy man," I declared.

Dragon grinned.

"Yeah, he's a machine, that one. Kitted out the whole club, everyone's rooms, and he still has enough to sell original furniture pieces online."

"Impressive," I murmured, running a fingertip along one of the live-edge shelves, letting my eyes wander the spines of the books housed there.

Dragon chuckled. "I figured that'd be the first place you went."

"You've an impressive library," I remarked. I needed my glasses to read some titles, but others stood out just fine.

He set my old-style carpet bag gently on the floor near an old black leather recliner and pulled the chain on the reading lamp that arched over it. The dimly-lit room was suddenly much better. I smiled and he went quietly to the door and eased it closed. Suddenly, it was just us.

"It's nice in here," I said, softly.

"It's just me an' Doc that live here full time," he said.

I raised my eyebrows.

"You live here!" I exclaimed, surprised.

He gave a single nod. "Goin' on a couple a years now. I turned mine and Tilly's house over to my boy, Dray, when Everett moved in. They needed a place of their own and it was only a little two-bedroom."

"Sounds cozy," I murmured.

He was stalking towards me, the sound of his boots muffled by the thick dark carpet.

"It was," he said. "But I like it here…" He pulled himself close, his hands sliding over my hips and along my lower back, one hand dipping lower to caress my ass. I swallowed hard, my body giving a throb of wanting I hadn't felt in a real long time.

"It's been a long time," I murmured, laughing a bit nervously. "I'm not real sure I remember how…"

"You ain't gotta do a thing, Sugar. I'm happy to do all the work," he said, his voice low in a sexy husky purr.

Oh, Lord have mercy! I am on board, yeee-haw! I thought, but his mouth was already gently tasting mine, my bottom lip lightly captured between his teeth. My arms had somehow made their way around his shoulders without me realizing it, and things were just naturally heating up, progressing from there.

I couldn't remember a time I'd ever been so turned on by a man, and it was kind of embarrassing to even admit that to m'self, having been married and with two beautiful daughters to show for it.

His lips lingered against mine, then moved to the side of my neck as he pulled me in close and I let my eyes drift shut, enjoying the closeness for just a moment before I let my damn nerves ruin everything…

"Wait, slow down," I murmured, and immediately felt defeat edged in regret.

"Not used to slow," he growled against my throat and I let my eyes slip shut again.

"And I ain't used to going so fast," I argued.

He stopped and drew back just enough to look at me, and when he did, he *really* looked at me. I felt like he saw me, and at the same time, saw right through me. His fingertips were gentle where they touched my cheek and he asked me, "What's really going on?"

I searched his face, trying to come up with anything but the truth because it was so stupid.

"Guilt, I think," I said, finally.

"Guilt?"

I sighed and took a short step back, nodding.

"Talk to me," he ordered gently, and I could tell I wasn't going anywhere until I came clean. In an echo of my thoughts, he said, "Ain't goin' nowhere until we have this talk, Marcie. What is it? What reason would you have to feel guilty?"

"Several, actually, and all of 'em are pretty stupid."

He chuckled and moved over to his recliner, dropping into it. I lowered myself onto the edge of the bed, facing him. There really wasn't anyplace else left to go.

"You're divorced, ain't yah?" he asked.

"Yes," I nodded.

"Still love him?" he asked.

"Yes," I said with a sigh, and all of those bleak feelings came rushing back.

"What happened?" he asked.

I swallowed hard.

"At first, it was work, then he'd rather be watching football, and then it was going out with the boys, and then, and then, and then... Eventually, it came down to it, he just weren't never home and even when he was, it was like he wasn't with me."

Dragon grunted and a somewhat pained look flashed in those dark eyes of his. He nodded and said, "Shift a woman to the back burner often enough, long enough, don't pay no mind to her and eventually she burns, just like anything else."

He was right. At first I'd cried. Then I'd twisted inside and become black and bitter. I hated myself, loathed the way I looked in my husband's eyes. I'd tried everything to fix myself for him... changed my hair, which he'd hated, lost weight, exercised more, even had considered surgery, but it was when I'd found another woman's lipstick on his collar that I realized the problem might not be with me.

Things had blown to high heaven when I confronted him, and a lot of hurtful shit had been said, and I called it quits. He didn't think I'd go through with it, but I did. My daughters had been so mad at him and me. Him, for being such a damn fool, and me, for being so unyielding, but I had to. Weren't no one going to respect me if I couldn't respect myself. I'd let that lapse for so long I still wasn't quite sure if I could do it.

Dragon sighed and shook his head when I finished unloading and handed me a bandana to wipe my nose with when I'd become tearful.

"That's a pretty big hurt you got there," he said finally, gently. "Do my best not to aggravate it and I can slow down if you need. For now, anyways."

"You sure?" I asked.

"I'm sure," he nodded. "Let's go wash your face and get you cleaned up some, baby. We can leave this at 'to be continued' for now."

I felt just awful about it, ruining what promised to be a good time with my insecurities, but I honestly was scared to death. I didn't know that I could live through another kind of hurt like I had with Bobby. I was beginning to love the lighthearted banter, the deep discussions with this man, but I was skittish and right shy about giving my whole heart over.

He walked me to the bathrooms and waited outside while I cleaned up, when I came out fresh-faced, he smiled and said, "Some reason, I like you better without makeup."

I laughed and said, "Pretty sure no one likes a woman my age without a little help from a bottle," I said.

"Ain't been drunk once any of the times I've kissed you," he murmured. "Ain't the least bit impaired now." He pulled me to him and kissed me gently. When he drew back it was only slightly and he whispered against my lips, "You're a beautiful woman, Marcie. Real, and tough." He chuckled, drawing back a little further, "Real tough, too. I like that about you."

"You know just what to say to make a girl's heart flutter," I told him and he winked at me.

"Biker's got charm, eh?"

"Some real smooth moves," I agreed.

He chuckled and led me down the hall toward a door, green grass beyond the window set in it.

"I still got plenty in my bag of tricks," he said.

I smiled, I couldn't help it.

"I'll just bet you do…"

15

D ragon…

One of the biggest fights I'd ever had with my wife was over what Marcie had just described. I'd made that mistake once and only once. Neglect, even benign, could be so damaging a person couldn't ever recover. I could see now that Marcie was one of those people. Can't say I blamed her none, and it was a damn shame. She had a heart of gold. The more I learned about her, the more my feelings deepened and it felt good. Nice, actually.

I wasn't in any hurry. If it was slow she needed, the ability to build trust, I could give that to her. Anything good in the world that came your way was worth waiting for. Worth nurturing and growing… Tilly had taught me that, too, with her garden and her roses, with her infinite patience with my fuckups. I missed her, I always would, but any time I thought along the lines that I may be betraying her or her memory somehow, the smell of roses like to knock me on my ass and I had to take it as the sign it was.

My dead wife approved, and if I didn't follow through, she'd like to kick my ass when I got to the other side. Tilly and Marcie had that in common. They were both real tough and they weren't afraid of being hard as diamond if and when they needed to be. It was on me not to give 'em a reason to harden up and shut me out.

That's where Marcie's generosity came in. She was generous to a fault, from what I'd learned, and that generosity extended to second, third, fourth, and maybe even as far as fifth chances. She was downplaying things with her ex-husband. She had to be. Kind of boggled my mind that even after all of that, she still managed to stay friends with him. Folding up and putting away her hurt even from that? Well, that was the mark of a remarkable woman. Still, my heart hurt for her; it hurt even more knowing the damage that Duracell caused with his final words, and that those same words were coming back to haunt her even now.

She was half a step behind me when we got to the window, so I saw Blue and Hayley, and their little boy, Damon, on the lawn a second before she did. She gave a sharp tug on my hand, our interlocked fingers tangling. I turned back to look into her startled, fearful blue eyes and I smiled reassuringly.

"It's okay, Sugar. You knew this day would come when you started seein' me." I pulled her gently along up to my side, and she wrapped both her arms around my one and hugged it.

It reminded me of a small girl with her teddy bear, comin' out of her room in the middle of the night, scared from a bad dream.

Made me realize that maybe she'd let herself fool herself into thinking this thing we had startin' up between us was nothing but a dream at all, and seeing that little guy with the crown of red curls with his dark-haired mother and his brunette father drove that home. Reality came crashing in and her nerve was faltering, but I wouldn't let her fall.

As far as that boy knew, he had two loving parents. As far as that man was concerned, he was that boy's father. As far as Hayley and Blue and the loss of their third? They knew. They knew that it was for the best. They knew that Cell was poison and that he would have destroyed them all, eventually. They knew, and the pain of that realization had dulled some with time, but it would never fully go away.

Pain was Duracell's legacy and while I loved him as a brother, I hoped he burned in Hell for it.

Marcie, to her credit, stood a little straighter, her chin raising marginally, her gait even with mine, even as Blue paused and looked us over as we approached the blanket his wife sat on with his son. He gave a careful nod, light gray eyes studying Marcie, a slight frown of concentration creating a little line between his eyebrows as he took my new lady's measure.

"Ma'am, it's nice to see you again," he said softly, with a polite nod.

"Oh, hello!" Hayley said warmly, her hand to her forehead, shading her eyes as she peered up at us both. Damon echoed his mother, staring up at Marcie curiously, drool coating his little chin.

"What a beautiful baby," Marcie said with a sweet smile, and lookin' at Damon, it was hard not to let your heart melt. He was a beautiful boy, with all his biological father's good looks and charm. It was still too early to tell, but I had a good feeling that was where the similarities to Cell were gonna end: with that shock of red hair and his sperm donor's good looks.

Personality-wise, I saw him already as a true cross between his sweet mother and thoughtful father, Blue. I had high hopes that the kid was gonna be just fine, and with the club there to catch him and keep him straight, I had no real worries about it. Still, I knew his parents did and I also knew they weren't gonna relax until he was of an age where we could all tell for sure what he was gonna be like.

I was glad to see that meeting up with Blue and Hayley again wasn't too big a deal for Marcie or for them. I was even happier to see that meeting Damon for the first time hadn't shook Marcie overly much. His sweet baby smile was hard to feel sorrow or remorse around, though.

We stood and visited a while before moving over to the swings around Rush's fire-pit. An amazing structure, hand-built and carved by the man, it was one of my favorite places in the clubhouse, which was coming into its own nicely through the love of its brothers and women. It helped that money didn't seem to be no object no more, thanks to Ashton and Shelly, Ashton for the start-up funds and Shelly due to her sheer magic with bookkeeping and investments.

That woman was a maverick with a calculator and calculated risks.

I'd be lyin' if I said I didn't miss fuckin' her. She'd been a lot of fun before what happened, and now, she was getting back to that fun-loving woman, although in a much different direction now that she was a mamma. Swear to god, Ghost needed to stay off of her for a minute to let her recover between kids some. She always did want a big family, though, so it might not have been all on him. Lucky for her, her little ones had plenty of aunts and uncles to help out.

The brothers and sisters who had a chance to meet her took an immediate shine to Marcie. I was really only worried about one, though, and he had yet to make an appearance.

Think of the devil and he shall appear…

Marcie was lounging against me, the fire flickering, sunset past by an hour or so. Doc trudged across the gravel circle and dropped onto a swing next to ours, leaning back with a gusty sigh and propping his booted feet on the arm. I'd seen more than one of the boys sleep it off on one of the swinging benches, always wondered how they managed to lay on the damn things without spilling out and breaking their fucking head.

"What's up, Doc?" I asked.

"Long fuckin' day," he said, heaving out a gusty sigh. "I'm getting too old for this shit."

"Motherfucker, you're only seven years older 'n me."

"And I'm feelin' every one of 'em. To add insult to injury, somebody got my last MGD."

Marcie giggled and said, "That would be me, sorry about that. If I'd known, I would have asked for something else."

Doc chuckled and said, "Miller Genuine Draft, a classy lady like you? Never would have guessed it." He winked one blue eye at my girl and I think she blushed all the way to the roots of her copper dye-job.

"Classy? Huh…" She started laughing and sighed happily, saying, "I didn't know any better, I'd say you're so full of shit your eye were brown."

Doc laughed and I laughed too. "Told you she was a firecracker."

"That you did, compadre. That you did," Doc agreed cheerfully. Then he got solemn. "I hate to say it, but I don't think I'm gonna make this run."

"Oh?" I asked.

He shook his head. "Hospital is short-staffed and it just wouldn't be right, leavin' knowing I got patients, you know?"

"Well, sure," Marcie said. "Though I'm sad I won't get to know you right away."

"Aw, hell, gettin' to know me is the *last* thing you'd wanna do, darlin'. I'm just a dirty old man."

Marcie laughed and I shook my head.

"You're sure, now?"

"Hell, yes, I'm sure," Doc grumbled. "Besides, God knows I love all that have gone before, but I just don't know that I got it in me to sit through the tributes this year."

He looked so tired, then; unhappy. I understood. In years past, I'd felt the same, but I never missed a Lake Run. Kind of hard to when you were the president. As for Doc, he wasn't an officer no more, heading into a semi-retired status within the club, enjoying just being a member for the time being. I could tell he was asking me for my blessing on this, and I could also tell he needed it. I gave him a nod over Marcie's head where it rested on my shoulder and chest and said, "Your patients and the citizens of this town need to come first. You've always been a doctor first."

"Not always," he disagreed. "Not in my view. Just, this weekend, I need to be. We got one doc down with a shoulder injury, one down with a staph infection, and our nursing staff is at an all-time low. Hospital is running on a shoe-string budget and it's starting to show."

"Why's it so bad?" Marcie asked.

"Hm," Doc hitched back and said, "Folks around these parts are poor. Hospital bills don't get paid, mismanagement, it's always been a small town rural hospital... kind of a perfect storm, really... but you don't want to hear about all that."

He made a start to heave himself back onto his tired feet, wincing, and said, "I'm going to drag these old bones into a hot shower and into bed," then sank back into the chair with a grunt. "In just a minute."

"All right, brother," I murmured, worried for my old friend. He'd been working himself nigh to the bone lately. Going through a lot of the same motions I had, after Tilly. Only problem was, I knew firsthand this was the kind of shit you had to feel on your own. No one could relate, no one could know how it felt for you, even if they'd been through it. No one had been able to really help me through my grief in the beginning, not until I let them. As a result, I just plain didn't know how to help my friend through his, even though I'd been there myself, feeling exactly what he was feeling.

Truth was, Doc had helped me, plenty of times. I'd returned the favor where I could, it just never felt like it was enough. Hell, it could never *be* enough. Not for something like this.

I was distracted by a contended but tired sigh from Marcie, who struggled to sit up. I smiled and asked, "That my cue that it's time for bed?"

She snorted, "For me, yes, but you're a grown-ass man. You go on and do what you want."

I think I fell a little bit in love with the woman right then, because the keen look she gave me said, '*Stay out here and tend to your friend if he or you needs it.*' I checked with Doc with a look, but he was already drowsing by the light of the fire. I shook my head and got up with her.

"Doc, old friend, I think it's time for you to hit the hay."

He startled a bit and rubbed the back of his bald head.

"I think you're right," he said with a sigh. I held out a hand and hauled him up to his feet. He winced and squeezed my hand a couple of times.

"Y'all ride safe now, y'hear?" he asked when we reached the back door.

"Loud and clear, buddy. You keep the dirty side down, yourself."

"Will do," he said and slipped into his room, shutting the door softly behind him.

I turned to Marcie, who I had tucked under one arm. She looked to me and I smiled and asked, "Ready for take two?"

"As much as I'd love to go there with you, liquid courage on board and all, I'm ready for *bed*."

She looked it, too, tiredness radiating from her. Probably a little more mental and emotional than physically, but it didn't really matter. Tired was tired, and I could respect it, even if I didn't like it much. My cock was pretty much at attention any time I looked at her anymore.

"Come on, I'll read you a bedtime story," I murmured.

She smiled and the joy that was in it made me ache to be inside her. She became a special kind of beautiful when she smiled like that.

"I'd really like that," she said and I pressed my lips against her temple, breathing in her soft, womanly scent.

She wanted slow and easy, I could give it to her, regardless of if I was used to it or not. It really wasn't asking all that damn much of me, which I could appreciate about her. She didn't ask for anything, really. It was a rare quality in a woman. *Lucky for me finding it twice*, I thought.

I tried not to compare Marcie to Tilly, but sometimes it happened. I struggled a bit inside, but every time I came anywhere close to cold feet or felt like I was somehow betraying my wife...

"Whew," Marcie remarked, breaking me out of my thoughts. "Girl, you're supposed to wear your perfume, not bathe in it."

"What's that?" I asked, opening up my room's door.

"Don't you smell that?" she asked.

I shook my head.

"Smells like roses," she said, and I smiled.

16

Marcie…

I slipped back into his room from changing in one of the bathrooms. I know, I know! I shouldn't care, but this man made my heart flutter and gave me butterflies in my stomach and for some reason, I just got so damn *nervous* and I know I wasn't no beauty queen no more. My stomach wasn't flat, my tits weren't perky, and I had more cellulite than any woman would be proud of, but still… when he looked up at me over the top of his simple black-framed reading glasses, I was that same kind of torn I had been earlier.

Do I stay or do I go? Am I ready to share this man's bed, even just for sleeping? Oh, God, Marcie! Get a grip, woman!

"What's wrong?" he asked softly and I slowly set my belongings onto the recliner.

"Just," I cleared my throat, it was suddenly almost too tight to talk. "Sorry, just nervous, I guess."

His dark eyes raked me from head to toe. "I like it," he said.

"What? This old thing?" It was a simple country nightgown I'd ordered out of the Vermont Country Store catalog ages ago and one of my favorites, a simple tank-top design up top flowing into an almost-floor-length dress. White cotton with eyelet lace accents. It was cool in the summer time and with the weather getting warmer... *Yeah right, the heat in here has nothing to do with the weather.*

"Looks nice on you. Would look better on my floor, but we'll get there in good time."

I blushed and waved a hand in front of me laughing, and he smiled, looking delicious sitting up in bed, the blankets at his hips, his tattooed and muscled chest on display.

"Come here," he ordered softly, and it sent a thrill down my spine. He wasn't asking, and I wasn't about to get *that* shy on him. I went around to the side of the bed he'd left vacant for me and he threw back a triangle of blankets to let me get in. Of course, I froze when I realized he wasn't wearing anything.

"You always sleep in the nude?" I asked.

"Usually. Now get in and come here. I believe I promised you a bedtime story."

"I believe you did," I said, and I swear I could barely breathe.

I got in and he pulled me close. I cuddled into his side and kept my arm over his lean hips well above and out of the way of his penis.

Lord have mercy, woman. Since when did you turn into such a prude?

He put his arm around me and cuddled me close and I loved it. It felt safe in his arms, despite his and his club's reputation... or maybe, if I were being honest, because of it. He lifted the paperback we'd been reading together and I closed my eyes, resting my cheek against his warm skin, as his rough, yet melodic voice picked up where we last left off.

He stopped after a time and I opened my eyes and looked up. His smile was gentle, his eyes kind, and he said, "Thought you was asleep."

"No, not yet."

"You want I should read more?"

I wanted that he should kiss me. He must have read it in my face because he set the book aside and did just that. My heart was in my throat as his lips moved against mine and I closed my eyes again. For a man his age, he moved lightning fast, and pressed me back into the sheets, his hands at my hips, raising my nightgown, but after having listened to him – reading a romance no less– I was aroused. Wet and wanting, my nervousness waning when he didn't make to uncover us or take off my clothes.

He knelt between my thighs and growled by my ear, "You want I should put on a condom?"

"What for?" I asked breathlessly. "Can't get pregnant."

"There's other reasons for a condom, you know," he murmured against the side of my neck.

"You got something I need to know about?"

"No."

"Then shut up and get to fuckin'," I ordered with a false bravado, but hey, fake it 'til you make it, right?

I grasped his face between my hands and dragged his mouth back to mine. The head of his cock nudged against the inside of my thigh and I spread my legs for him. He nudged against my sex and I moaned, feeling like I would die if he didn't get himself inside me sooner rather than later.

He wasn't gentle, but he was restrained, if that made sense. He took me at my word and pressed into me, and it felt so good I pressed my body down to meet his upward thrust. I bit my bottom lip to muffle the cry that came out of me and he stilled. He looked down at me, sweetly and tenderly caressing my face, and asked, "Did I hurt you?"

I shook my head and dragged his mouth to mine again, wrapping my legs around him under the tangle of blankets and sheets. He groaned into my mouth and thrust, and I moaned into his, right back.

Our breathing quickened, my pulse flashing like lightning, pushing the blood through my veins and vaporizing me from the inside out with pleasure as he found a steady drag and thrust that moved over everything important on the inside. The euphoria rose steadily, along with my hips off the bed, as I tried to meet him half way. His cock hit my cervix just right in that sweet flash of pain that dissolved like cotton candy on the tongue into an erotic bliss.

"That's it, baby. Come for me," he murmured in my ear, his breath hot against my neck, my body tightening at the rough quality of his voice, full of lust and need. "Oh, yeah! Tighter," he growled and I tensed my pelvic muscles even more for him. He groaned and drove into me that one final time that sent me sailing over the cliff. I cried out and held onto him as I felt like I was falling forever, and then I landed, the shock of it all overwhelming to the point that tears sprang to the corner of my eyes.

Dragon held me close, panting, making soothing noises, until my body stopped trembling beneath his. He chuckled when I pulled his mouth to mine and kissed him with a desperate passion and when he pulled back just enough to see me, he winked and said, "Looks like I've still got it."

I laughed and hugged him with my whole body, and said, "I'll say!"

"There's plenty more where that came from, Sugar, but we've got a long ride tomorrow. I don't want to break you and I definitely want to save you for later." He kissed me, and the way he swept his tongue against mine, the moan he let out, it was like he couldn't get enough of me. *Me, a little ol' small town housewife and he's treating me like a rare piece of candy to be savored and saved for later.*

I don't think I'd ever been treated like that before, in all the time I'd been married. It was visceral and very emotional for me, and of all the men in the world to make me feel that way...

"Talk to me," he murmured, and swept a thumb through the moisture at the corner of my eye, near my temple.

"You really know how to treat a woman," I whispered and he chuckled.

"Surprised?" he asked, and slid from my body with a shudder and a groan.

"It that awful of me?" I asked meekly, not wanting to hurt his feelings.

He chuckled again and lay back down next to me, his hand trailing over my nightgown, skittering up my inner thigh in a way that made me shiver before he cupped my pussy with his hand.

"What are you doing?" I asked.

"You," he said and slid his fingers where his cock had been moments before. I shivered and bit my lower lip. "I wanna watch you come for me," he said and I swallowed hard.

"Didn't you just?"

"Yeah, but I wanna see it again, and then, maybe again after that."

"I thought you didn't want to leave me sore."

"Guess you better make this orgasm a good one, then." His grin was wolfish and I thought to myself that maybe, just maybe, I'd bitten off a little more than I could chew with the biker.

"I guess you better give me something to really come for," I shot back and his smile grew.

"Challenge accepted," he whispered and found that spot inside me with his fingers while he planted his thumb firmly against my clit.

Oh god, definitely more than I could handle.

He must have read it on my face because he put his lips against my ear and whispered, "Next time you tell me to get to fuckin', maybe you'll remember who's in charge."

I laughed then, and – big mistake. The man was just as good with his fingers as he was his dick, and he wasn't going to let up until I begged for him to stop.

17

D^{ragon...}
"Watch where you're goin,' you fat old bitch!"

The young buck shoulder-checked Marcie comin' out the diner's front door hard enough to send her into a spin, her hip slamming painfully into the railing on the edge of the front stoop. I knew it hurt, because she cried out.

So did the young buck when he reached the bottom of the stairs and his face crashed into my fist. I'd cocked back and followed through beautifully. His jaws clacked together as he rocked back, lost balance, and went down on his ass on the steps leading up into our mid-way lunch spot.

Marcie jumped and cried out again, her hands flying to her mouth as I reached down and helped the boy up, clapping my hands down onto his shoulders, balling my fists into his lapels. I stood him up and brought him eye-to-eye with me.

"I do believe you just got owned by some instant karma here, boy. Now apologize to my lady."

If he didn't apologize, I was liable to belt him again. He glared at me, but with Trig stepping up at my back along with Reaver, he finally registered he was on the losing end here. Trig loomed, and the guy shrank in my hands.

He cocked his head and looked up in Marcie's direction.

"Sorry, lady," he mumbled.

I shook him, "'Ma'am', and you'd better do better n' that."

"Dragon –" Marcie started, and I silenced her with a look.

"No way, baby. You don't get disrespected in my presence. That's not how this life works. He disrespects you, he disrespects *me;* and I won't be disrespected."

I gave him a little shake and he swallowed hard, a knot already comin' up on his jaw. He said, "I apologize, Ma'am. Please forgive me."

"Ain't her forgiveness you need, boy. It's mine, and I ain't the forgivin' type. Get the fuck on outta here." I tossed his ass in the direction of the lot, where several good ol' boy pickups were backed into spaces and he stumbled. He caught himself and slunk through the gauntlet of black leather and angry men from the club. The women, to their credit, stood aside, subdued, wrangling their children.

Data took a picture of the boy getting into his truck and called out, "Got your license plate. Call the cops, they'll never find your body," he declared. Mali laughed and it was an evil sound. I matched it with a nasty smile.

"He ain't gonna do shit," I called. "He's gonna take his lesson and get on with his life, ain't yah, boy?"

He gave a nod, his face pale, and started up his truck and drove away.

"Still keepin' the picture," Data called back.

"Expect nothin' less," I said, and rubbing the knuckles on my hand, I turned back to Marcie. Her expression was clouded with some unnamed emotion and I went to her, hooking an arm around her shoulders I gave her a side-hug and put a quick kiss to her temple.

"You okay?" I asked, dropping my hand to her hip.

"Might be bruised in the mornin', but I'm alright," she murmured. I opened the diner's door for her and she stepped through.

"Sorry you had to deal with that asshole," I said.

"Didn't have the chance," she said, pointedly.

I chuckled and nodded, "You're right, I didn't give you the chance. I just reacted. I won't apologize for it."

"No, I don't suppose you would," she said, but she didn't sound happy about it. I let it go, the mood suddenly tense between us. She still had a lot to learn about this life, about how we didn't play by citizen rules. It wasn't a conversation for a diner full of those citizens, nor was it a conversation for in front of my brothers. It was a conversation for between just me and her, so I let the tension between us slide, glad for it that no one seemed to notice it, with a mind to remedy it as soon as possible, once we got to the lake.

She was quiet in that way that told me I was damn sure in some hot water with her, but like me, she would wait until we was in private to discuss it. Despite being quietly angry at me, she was pleasant to everyone else. Maybe a little more so to the owners and waitstaff of the establishment we was dining in.

Before we got back on the road, I went back to take a piss and ran into my son coming out the john. He smirked at me and I grinned back and said, "Say what's on yer mind, boy."

"She's heated; I am glad I am not you right now."

I chuckled and shook my head, saying, "She ain't that hot, but she do have the same look as yer mother."

He leaned against the wall in the narrow hall and smiled, but it was edged in pain. He nodded and said, "The quieter she got, the more pissed she was."

I nodded. "I think it's just a female thing, ain't specific to just one of 'em."

"I do believe you're right. Sometimes it's like they're a whole other species."

I laughed at that, and said, "To be fair, the fact that they get quiet and suppress things – I think that shit's our fault."

"My, how feminist of you," he said, and grinned.

"It ain't really. It's just the goddamned truth."

He scowled a little and nodded. "It makes sense," he agreed. "Still ain't going to figure out all their deal, though."

I laughed. "Never. I wouldn't even hazard a guess on half the shit they get up to or what they got going on in their heads."

"It's probably all our fault, somehow," he smirked.

"Most of the time, yeah. All of the time? I think that's a bit of a reach. Now get outta my way, I gotta piss."

"Pipe getting leaky in your old age?" he asked, pushing off the wall.

"Keep talkin' like that, son, your balls are gonna be shoved so far into your body cavity you ain't ever gonna have to worry about 'em gettin' saggy."

He trailed up the hall laughing his ass off, and I went in and did my business.

She was quiet, with a tight-lipped smile when I got out to the bike. Climbed on behind me without a word and cuddled up to my back, so she was miffed, but cooled off enough from her mad.

I'd figured as much, but I still wasn't lookin' forward to the talk.

Who knew? Maybe it wouldn't be all that bad. If it were Tilly, I'd have just fucked her brains out and that would have been the end of it, but Marcie wasn't Tilly, and Marcie wasn't the type to let sex distract her.

I shouldered the bags and reached a hand out when we parked at the lodge. She hesitated for only a second, her expression softening into something like hurt, and took the hand I offered. I brought it to my lips and kissed it firmly, and without a word to the rest, led her around the side of the main lodge to the path leading down to the cabin. She followed me, and I warned her to watch her step when I found one of the pavers of one of the steps in the path was loose.

Mad at me or not, I wasn't the type of asshole that wouldn't take care of his woman. I never had been and I never would be.

When we reached the cabin that served as home base for the officers and their women on Lake Run, I dragged the old, creaky screen door open and ushered her into the living room. She looked it over, and smiled, charmed, and I led her to the first room across from the entryway and through the door. She shut it behind us and I waited her out, patiently,to let her have her say.

"I can take care of myself, you know," she said finally, and she sounded offended.

I nodded.

"I know that, Sugar, and I would have let you handle it, *if* he'd left it at words. He didn't; he shoved you, and so he needed put in his place."

"Just like that?" she asked.

I nodded, "Just like that. He disrespected you past what any of me or mine could tolerate and I'm tellin' you, he got off easy." I went to her and rested my hands gently on her hips and brought her in close. "I know you can take care of yourself, baby. Trust me on that. What I did wasn't because you couldn't, what I did was because you shouldn't have to. Not with me around to take care of you."

She searched my face, her blue eyes wide and turning slightly glassy with unshed tears. It hurt me, surprisingly deep, that she'd felt all alone for so long. I'd gathered that her ex was apathetic on a good day, but Goddamn. No woman who is with any kind of real man should be assaulted and verbally abused in front of him and still have to handle the situation on her own. That shit just wasn't right. Of course, I could be off-base, judging a man and a situation I knew nothing about… but I didn't think I was too far left or right of the centerline on this one.

"I ain't used to anyone lookin' out for me," she said, her voice holding a fine tremble to it.

I smiled and kissed her sweet, whispering against her lips, "Good thing I'm stickin' around for you to get used to it, huh?"

"Whatever shall I do?" she whispered back.

I grinned slyly against her lips.

"Can start with a 'Thank you'."

Her lips curled against mine and she giggled, her breath fanning warm against my lips. She asked me, "And what form would you like that 'Thank you' to take?"

"Preferably, one where yer on your knees with my dick in that soft mouth of yours." I pressed my thumb against her bottom lip and with her sultry bedroom gaze she lapped at it with her tongue. Fuck, that was some hot shit. My cock went from zero to sixty in less than half a second.

She stared me in the eye, all trace of shyness gone from her as she went for my chaps. She worked the front of 'em open, then went for the belt underneath, her deft fingers peeling off the layers until she was stroking me, her fingers gentle but firm around my shaft.

She lowered herself to the edge of the bed, leading me around by the balls, which she fondled perfectly with her other hand, and without much fanfare, took the head of my cock between those silky soft lips and plunged her wet, hot mouth over me, taking me all the way into the back of her throat.

That shit was damn near porn-star perfect and sexy as hell. I closed my eyes and threw back my head while her perfect mouth worked my cock, and shuddered, damn near losing my mind when she moaned around it, the vibrations of that sultry sound shaking me to the core, rocking my world.

"Up, get up," I gasped in a strained voice.

She released my cock from her mouth with an adorable little 'pop' and stood up. I made quick work of getting her pants and panties down and spun her around, shoving her over the bed, forward onto her hands. I let my fingers delve into her velvet folds and found her wet and wanting. She moaned and ground her pussy back onto my hand, but I wanted my dick there. If she was gonna fuck me, I was gonna get something out of it, too.

I thrust into her tight wet heat and I wasn't gentle about it. She gasped, sharply and moved forward to ease things some, but once I was in all the way, she rocked her hips back to take me in further. I smiled and said, "Hang on, baby, I'm takin' you on the ride of your life."

I fucked the shit out of her. By the time I really got going, I discovered there was more than just her blowjobs that was porn-star perfect about her. She really let go this time, her fingers gripping the quilt on the bed with one hand, the other she slicked through her wetness and teased her own clit while I pounded into her from behind. Each thrust dragged a ragged gasp of breath out of me, each sharp report of my flesh against hers whipped me into a deeper frenzy. Each cry, each moan that she let out, drove me into a pure sort of madness that made me want to give her more.

I guess I was wrong. I guess sex worked just fine when it came to Marcie Lanham and taking her mind on to other things.

18

M arcie...

It was beautiful here. The boys in the club were rowdy, exuberant, and insistent that everyone join in the fun, but no one seemed to mind none when I took myself down to the little beach and walked a bit away from everybody. The sun was setting, the fiery pinks and oranges reflected in the rippling waters, as I dug my toes into the smooth pebbles and sand of the lakeshore and I just took a moment of peace for myself. I wasn't a partier, never really had been, and sometimes I just needed to take a breather for myself.

I closed my eyes and listened to the water lap the shore, and remembered when my kids were just kids, probably five or six, how we'd gone all the way out to South Carolina to see some distant relatives of Bobby's for some family reunion. The sun was shining; it was a rare day, the girls were actually getting along. the two of them crafting sandcastles and decorating them with bits of pretty rock they found and the occasional seashell. I'd lounged in the sun reading, and Bobby had brought me the occasional glass of lemonade and had just let me read. It was one of my most favorite and cherished memories and I had to say, standing here like this, right now, I had the same sense of calm peacefulness. The same sort of all-was-right-with-the-world kind of satisfaction that I'd found was all too rare for me.

I turned and looked at the sound of approaching footfalls, the sound of sand and gravel half-sloshing, half-crunching beneath bootsoles, and saw Dragon resolutely marching up the shore in my direction, a cold bottle of my favorite beer in one hand and a bottle of his favored Corona in the other. He held out the MGD in my direction and I took it from him.

"You doin' all right, Sugar?" he asked me softly and I nodded, turning and trailing up the beach to a fallen log that was begging for me to have a seat. Dragon fell into step beside me and asked, "It's not gettin' to be too much for you, is it? I know the boys can get kind of rowdy when they cut loose."

I smiled and shook my head, "Oh, no. Not at all," I said. "Just taking a bit of a breather and gettin' a little nostalgic while I was at it."

"Oh, yeah? How's that?" he asked, sitting down beside me on the fallen log. I took a drink of my beer, savoring it a moment before swallowing slowly.

"Just remembering this one time Bobby and I took the girls to the Carolina coast. The sound of the water reminded me, sort of. Was one of my first times at the ocean, myself... The girls built sandcastles and I just lounged in the sun reading. It was nice. Peaceful-like. I been gettin' the same feeling here."

"Is that right?" he asked, and sounded pleased.

I knocked my shoulder into his.

"How about you?" I asked.

"Honestly," he said quietly, "this is the most at-peace I've felt in a long time."

"Yeah?"

"Yeah. I more n' kind of like it, too."

"Anything that could make it better?" I asked.

"Be kind of nice if we could stop with the pretendin' to be 'just friends' and move the relationship up a notch," he said.

I chuckled, "Pretty sure we took care of that when we started fuckin."

He smiled and reached up a hand, grazing my cheek lightly with his thumb. "Didn't want to take nothin' for granted," he said softly. "Quickest way to foul things up."

I nodded slowly, "It can be."

He smiled and it made him go from handsome to just plain hot.

"So, whaddaya say? Wanna be my girlfriend?"

I giggled and said, "Isn't there supposed to be some kind of note with a 'check yes or no' along with that question?"

"No paper layin' around except for one of your books and that right there would be sacrilege."

"Damn right it would be!" I cried.

He leaned in and kissed me. and I swear, I swooned.

"Didn't answer my question," he whispered against my lips as he drew back.

"I thought it was a given," I said. "I'm here, aren't I?"

"I'll be honest with you, Marcie. After my wife died, I had a lot of hard thinkin' to do." He turned away from me a little and narrowed his eyes, gazing out across the lake. I didn't say anything, just left my silence as an open invitation for him to speak his mind.

"I realized just how much I took that woman for granted in a lot of things, how much shit I pulled that just wasn't fair to her. How often I let her down and wasn't there when she needed me and how many times she was there for me despite it." He looked at me, his dark eyes raw and filled with pain, hardening as he issued his promise… "I swear to you, I'll never treat you that way."

"I appreciate that," I said, a bit breathlessly.

He twisted around on the log and lay down, using my lap as a pillow, resting his beer on his broad chest as he looked up at me. I combed my fingers through his hair and he closed his eyes, which made me smile. We sat like that, until the sun went down and I gave a little shiver from the chill now coming off the water. He opened his eyes and said, "Come on back to the cabin with me. I know just how to warm you up."

I smiled, a wry twist of my lips and said, "Oh, I'll just bet you do! Count me in."

He laughed and sat up and I stood, slowly. He took my empty bottle and his in one of his big hands, and my hand in his other, and we walked the path along the lakeshore that joined with the path leading to what he called the 'officer's cabin', which was separate from the main lodge and set back in the trees.

One of the men had his woman up against the wall beside the cabin's front door. I couldn't see who with the dark and distance, the porch-light illuminating them, but really, with the way he was kissing the side of her neck, the only thing really visible was her legs wrapped around his hips and that big ol' patch on his back, the human heart wrapped in barbed wire, the steel pipes belching their flames.

I hesitated, dragging on Dragon's hand and he chuckled and drew me up beside him. I bit my lips together and he whispered in my ear, "Just Trig and Sunshine. They like when people watch and will do it just about anywhere."

"Oh, my!" I felt myself blush and found myself wondering, once again, when the hell had I turned into such a prude?

I didn't think Dragon was too keen on letting me stay that way. He pulled me around in front of him, putting my back to his front, both of us facing the rutting couple on the porch. He rucked up my long skirt in the front, delving a hand down the front of my panties, his rough fingers stroking the lips of my sex, as I gasped quietly.

"You best look," he murmured darkly in my ear, his fingertips pressing just right into my clit, sending sparks of pleasure out from my center, turning up the heat just enough, just a little, to where I had to bite back a moan. He gently kicked my feet a little wider apart and massaged my pussy.

"That's my girl, I want you nice and wet for me," he crooned. His breath was hot against my neck, his teeth gently grasping my earlobe. A shot and shiver of desire went down my neck at the same time it came up from my core, and when it crashed in the middle I had to fight to keep quiet. Those two up on the porch mmight be into being watched, but I wasn't. I was definitely into watching, though. Especially with Dragon's fingers against me, working my own desire into a fevered pitch.

I shuddered against him, ached to have him inside me, gasped and panted as he brought me so maddeningly close but it wasn't going to be an orgasm that would be fulfilling in any kind of way. I was missing an important part of his anatomy for that. I needed to be stretched and filled by his cock when I came, I just did, and his keeping me out here, while scorching hot, just wasn't doing it for me.

"You need to take me inside," I demanded and he chuckled darkly.

"Guess you better come for me, Sugar. You come for me, I'll take you inside and fuck you until you beg me to stop. You come for me now, I'll give you more than you can handle, later."

"How about you give it to me now?"

"Greedy little thing, ain't yah?"

"You make me this way," I gasped as he drove his fingers deeper between the folds of my pussy lips, coating them in my wetness and slicking them up and over my clit. Fire raced through my veins and I gasped, biting down on my bottom lip to keep from moaning and drawing attention to ourselves. He pressed the front of himself against my ass and I could feel how hot and hard he was through the front of his jeans and the back of my dress.

I groaned as he worked my clit, worked me higher and higher. He encouraged me with fingers against my body, lips against my skin, breath against my neck, voice in my ear…

"Yeah, baby, that's my girl. Come for me, I wanna feel you shudder against me, I wanna feel you fall. I'll be right here to catch you, darlin', you can trust me on that."

I felt weak in the knees, something I had only experienced once or twice. It scared me, overwhelmed me; I didn't want to fall for real, but I wanted what he was asking me to do, so badly. I leaned against him heavily and it was as if he was a tree, solid, steadfast, and holding true to his promise. He was gonna catch me, there was no need to be afraid. The knowledge that I really could trust him in this was so powerful it shook me to my core, which gave an answering throbbing contraction.

The orgasm was swift and swept me off my feet. I sagged back against him and sighed out in a shuddering rush as he worked my body with his one hand, the other arm around me, holding me to him. He smiled against the side of my neck and whispered, "Yeah, that's it."

I smiled, too, and smartass that I am, said, "You better finish what you started, *inside,* if you know what I mean."

"Oh, you're gettin' fucked. I promise you that, Sugar."

He held onto me until I felt like I was sure enough on my feet. By the time my dress dropped back down around my legs, the couple on the porch were disappearing inside. We waited a few moments before going in ourselves.

The common area of the large cabin was empty, and giggling like teens about to get caught, we dashed into his room where my laughter died on a soft surprised moan at the intensity with which he kissed me.

19

D ragon...

We lay in the dark, Marcie satiated for now, me likewise. She was dead asleep against my chest, curled into my side as I lay on my back, idly touching her soft skin with my rough fingertips. I sighed, slightly unsettled and having no reason as to really why, when a familiar voice from the past spoke from beside the window.

"I thought you didn't do guilt."

I blinked and looked over, the moonlight falling through the ancient glass painting her face a whiter shade of pale. Of course, it could just be that I was projecting. I mean, she *was* dead.

"Dreaming, aren't I?" I grunted.

"Yes and no," she said and pushed her hip off the wall, her arms falling to her sides. She was as achingly beautiful as she had ever been, my Tilly, her long dark hair falling in a straight cascade down her back, her lips their usual ruby red, her dark eyes perfectly lined in kohl, wide and vibrant.

"I swear, I will always miss you, baby," I murmured, the vision of her blurring with the sudden onset of my tears, which left me asking myself if it really were a dream or not. I mean, could you weep in a dream?

She chuckled and walked up, kneeling beside the bed close to me. I turned my head carefully. I didn't want to wake Marcie. Tilly folded her arms on the mattress and laid her head on them, bringing herself eye-to-eye with me.

"Finding any kind of love again isn't a betrayal, my love," she whispered.

I closed my eyes, the familiar fractured ache of grief and loneliness, of heartache and longing rising, fierce, and choking me up.

"I hurt you so bad." I couldn't help the broken in my voice. I couldn't do anything except be raw and honest in this moment.

She smiled at me sadly and reached out, trailing her fingertips through my tears.

"You also brought me the greatest joy in my life; don't sell yourself short. It. Wasn't. Your. Fault. You didn't make the decisions alone. I was a part of everything that was the club just as much as you were. I'm so sorry I left you and Dray, but I'm also so proud of the men you've both become."

She cradled my cheek and I turned my lips into her palm, pressing my lips to her cool skin, breathing in the roses she so loved.

"I still feel so lost without you, Babe."

She laughed lightly, "You were always the man with the plan, Baby. You always knew what direction to go. Never zigged when you should have zagged, and this is no different. I am happy for you; I *like* her, and I know you like her too. It may not be the same kind of love, but it *is* love just the same, and you deserve that happiness. You have my blessing. I don't know how much clearer I need to be that I approve and I'm afraid this is my last ditch effort to get you to see some fucking reason. She's good for you. You're good for each other... and I'm afraid you're going to need each other until the very end."

"What's that supposed to mean?" I asked.

She shook her head gently. "I've already said too much, and my time is pretty much up."

"Shit, so soon?"

She rolled her eyes. "I'm not even supposed to be here in the first place. Be glad I don't follow the rules."

It was my turn to smile. "You never did."

"No, I never did." Her lips curved into the most beautiful smile. It dazzled me, and I just wanted to hold her.

She leaned forward and pressed her lips to mine. I closed my eyes and kissed her back, her lips cold, her lipstick waxy. And when I opened my eyes again, she was gone.

I let my head fall back to the pillow and stared down at Marcie's peaceful slumbering face.

Tillly was right. It wasn't the same kind of love, but it was love. I had feelings for Marcie. Where with Tilly, it'd been all fire and passion, with Marcie it was a slower, gentler companionship that was steadily growing into something more. Blooming, like one of Tilly's roses, into something beautiful and full of life, just not wild. Something cultivated and cultured with care.

"You alright?" she murmured sleepily and I jumped.

"Yeah, why?" I asked, alarmed.

"Think you was dreamin'," she said.

"Something like that."

"Mm." She cuddled closer, and I held her tight and pressed a kiss to the top of her head. She sighed out contentedly and I felt a certain sort of elation before I closed my eyes and went to sleep myself.

Letting go was never fun, especially when you didn't really have a choice. Sometimes, though, it was a lot less scary to let go when you had something, or in this case, some*one* to grab onto.

SHE SEARCHED my face in the sunlight streaming through the window Tilly had been at the night before and took a breath to speak. She hesitated, closed her mouth, then thought better of it and spoke her mind.

"I don't think it was a dream," she said, finally. "And I don't think you're crazy. I mean, I've smelled roses around you, too. I had no idea your wife grew them, or that there was any significance to it."

"Is it bad that all I'm feelin' right now is relieved you don't think I'm nuts?"

Marcie laughed and cupped my cheek, she leaned in and kissed me gently, chastely, the same way Tilly had the night before. I closed my eyes, glad she let her warm lips linger on my own.

She heaved a big sigh and said, "I can't imagine what you two had together," she said and sounded almost wistful. "I know I could never replace her, and I'm not going to try –"

"Now hold on there, no one said anything about any of that."

"I know y' didn't. You've never, not once, made me feel like I've been in competition with her, but… I don't know. I guess it's different when she shows up like that."

"I tell you what," I said, rubbing my eyes with forefinger and thumb. "I think that was it. Never had a goodbye kiss taste so much like goodbye."

"Guess she sealed things with it," she murmured.

I nodded and it was my turn to cup her cheek with my hand, smoothing a thumb back and forth, hoping she could feel how much I cherished what we had going on.

She sighed and her shoulders relaxed, her blue eyes slipping shut as she turned her face into my touch.

"I always thought love was love," I murmured. "And in some ways, it is… but I can honestly tell you…" I paused, thinking just how to word this so it was presented the way I intended and left no room for misunderstanding. "I can honestly tell you, I don't love her the same as I love you. It's different. It's good. It's probably one of the best things to happen to me yet."

It was all true, and it was also confusing, how a bastard like me could luck out so completely. I mean, I knew I wasn't deserving of all these second chances, but here we were all the same. Marcie traced her fingers over my face and I closed my eyes. I wasn't quite ready to get out of bed yet, and neither was anyone else, I reckoned. It was early yet by hard-partying biker standards. Wasn't biker morning 'til after noon. We lay in bed beside each other, facing one another. I'd been touching her lightly, tracing patterns on her exposed skin until goosebumps raised along her arms, and she'd unintentionally begun to mirror me.

It weren't doin' nothin' for her poor pussy if it needed a break, because her fingertips against my skin was arousing to say the least. My cock stirred beneath the sheet, standing at attention and beggin' to go home.

"I swear to god, man. You're insatiable!" Marcie cried when I slid across the crisp cotton sheets and pulled her to me.

"That's your fault," I growled and kissed her.

"How's that?" she demanded after letting out a gasp.

"Can't get enough of you," I rumbled against her throat, working my way down.

"How is that *my* fault?"

"Because you're you," I said, as if it were the only explanation ever needed, and to me it was. I took her nipple into my mouth and bit gently, suckling at it until she moaned.

"That doesn't make any sense," she said breathlessly.

"Makes all the sense in the world, if you're me."

She laughed which turned into a soft whimper when I slid my hand beneath the sheets and cupped her between her legs.

"You good to go or you need a break?" I growled against her breast. She hesitated too long and I chuckled and looked up. "I think I broke you."

"I'll mend," she said and color rose in her cheeks. I crawled up her body and put my mouth on hers. She kissed me back, her hands to either side of my face, her body bowing in my direction, telling me just how much she wanted me, but I wasn't aiming to hurt her, and I could stand to take a break for her comfort.

"So, what's the big plan for today?" she asked when we'd settled down some.

"Not sure, baby. Let's go find out…"

Turns out it was still too early for there to be a plan, which was pretty much what I figured. One of the irrefutable parallels between Tilly and Marcie was that neither one of 'em could sit still for long. They always had to be doing something or other, even when the goal was to relax and do nothing. For Marcie, doing nothing was pretty much the opposite of relaxing, so I tried to give the rest of the boys and girls of the club the time to sleep and put Marcie's ass to work making us some coffee in the cabin's kitchen.

I think she was happy to have even something so small to do.Me, I was just happy to be gettin' caffeinated. I tried to give Doc a call, to tell him about the crazy shit that'd been my morning, but he didn't answer.

I figured he was either coming off a shift, catching some Z's from his shift, or was on the ride back to the club, so I didn't sweat it. If he didn't answer, it was usually one of the three. I'd see him tomorrow, as soon as we got back.

Marcie placed a steaming, cracked ceramic mug on the battered kitchen nook table in front of me and another across from me at her seat. She didn't sit, though. Instead she drifted around the kitchen and was a beautiful sight. Her step was light as air as she breezed over the worn, golden wood floors, getting the sugar and cream from the fridge that was so old, it was close to being an icebox.

"Will you sit down?" I asked and she smiled.

"When I'm good 'n ready," she shot back and I chuckled.

She sat down with a satisfied sigh and doctored up her coffee while I sipped mine black, my fingers itching to reach for a smoke. I knew she didn't like it, and I was tryin' to cut back. She was right. I wasn't gettin' any younger and I wanted to watch my grandson get older. I didn't want to miss anything, and if it came down to missing his birthday or graduation? Well, I'd rather miss the fuckin' cigarettes. I'd had my fun.

"I'm impressed," she remarked and I looked at her from behind the rim of my mug.

"How's that?" I asked.

"You've been up this long and you haven't smoked."

"Tryin' to cut back."

"Oh, goodie. You need to, should have done it a long time ago."

I nearly choked on my coffee and laughed.

"Jesus, you're bossy," I teased.

"I am," she agreed. "And you need to listen to me more often."

"Yeah? Why's that?"

"You'll live a longer, happier life."

"Longer maybe. You sure about that last part, though?"

She swatted my shoulder lightly and I laughed again, shaking my head.

"Walked right into that, didn't I?" she asked.

"That you did."

"So," she said, sobering a bit. "Tell me about this tribute you all do, I mean, I don't know if I should be out there. I didn't really know…" her voice trailed off and she shifted on her seat uncomfortably, turning her head to look anywhere but at me. I reached out and covered her hand with my own. She looked back my way and I could see it in her eyes, that she was torn, that she didn't know what to do, and just how out of place she felt.

"We write down some things and fold them into paper lanterns, and at dark, we say some words and send 'em out over the lake. We remember our dead, pay our respects, our tributes; then we deal with it in our own ways the rest of the night. Some get to drinkin', some get to fuckin'…" I trailed off and shrugged my shoulder. Her eyebrow raised and she looked at me.

"And you?"

"Busted," I said with a reckless grin. "Used to be, I would get to drinkin', then I would get to fightin'."

"And what do you feel like doing this time?" she asked, with an answering wicked grin of her own.

"You don't mind, I'd rather get to fuckin' than fightin'. Or, at the very least, if we do fight, I'd like to fuck the rage right outta you."

She frowned. "Now what would we have to fight about?" she asked.

"Good point, let's skip that for later. Ain't no couple perfect, we'll fight someday I'm sure. For now, let's just keep it to straight fuckin', if'n you don't mind."

She laughed softly and said, "I don't mind that at all."

A shuffling footfall sounded behind us and Reaver walked in, shirtless, the button undone on his jeans, rubbing a knuckle into one of his wild blue eyes.

"There coffee?" he asked.

"There is," Marcie said, rising. "Want I should fix you a cup?"

"Hell, yeah. Anything I can do?"

"Yeah," I said dryly. "You can button yer pants and put a fuckin' shirt on, y' pasty-ass white boy."

"Man, fuck you," he said laughing, dropping into Marcie's vacant seat.

"You, Trig, Sunshine, and Doll have a foursome or somethin'?" I asked.

He grinned and said, "I wish. Doll and I crashed in Doc's old room."

I sighed. I missed having Doc as an officer. Felt like I hadn't quite lost my right hand, but I'd definitely lost a few fingers, with him dropping back down to just bein' a member. I understood it. Wasn't gonna be long that I'd pass the torch myself. I was hopin' the club would see fit to accept my son as the Pres. If they didn't, well, that was what it would be. I would try to hide my disappointment. Not in my boy, though. In my boys. My brothers went a different direction, it would surely be their loss. Dray would be a fine leader to 'em. Of course, I was more 'n a bit biased. I could own that.

I frowned and asked, "Where the fuck was Data and Mali?" I demanded. Since Data had taken over as secretary, he should've been in Doc's old room on account of it was his now, for him and his ol' lady.

"Fuck if I know. Last I saw they were skinny-dipping, fuckin' out in the lake."

I rolled my eyes and shook my head.

"I guess it don't matter anyhow," I said.

Marcie brought over a steaming mug and set it in front of Reave. Without thinking about it, I put my hands to her hips and guided her into my lap. Reave's eyebrows went up and he didn't bother hiding his smile. He sipped at the coffee and made a face, reaching for the creamer.

"You know how to make a cup of brew," he said. "Holy Christ."

"Pussy," Marcie said dryly and took a sip of hers.

I laughed and Reaver grinned and nodded.

"Oh, yeah, she's a keeper."

20

Marcie…

The day was an interesting one, that's for sure. Shooting, knife-throwing, trash talk a-plenty. Sunbathing, and reading idly by the lakeside watching the babies play. It was everything I needed to recharge my soul, and I was glad I came.

I was lounging in a chair on the sand and pebble beach, soaking up the sun with a book in my hands, when Dragon's boy dropped onto the sand beside my chair. He dusted off his hands and braced his forearms on his knees, and stared, squinting, out over the water for a minute.

I didn't know what he wanted, or what to say, so I simply closed my book and laid it in my lap and waited. He raked his bottom lip between his teeth and sighed.

"I'd be lying if I said this wasn't awkward for me," he said, finally.

I nodded and said, "I can see that."

"He likes you – a lot. I haven't ever seen him look at anyone other than my mom the way he's been looking at you this weekend. I mean, it's not completely the same, but it's there. And I'm struggling."

I was impressed. Most men wouldn't admit that. Especially one as young as Dray. I folded my hands on top of my closed book and asked, "What do you think it would take to make this easier on you?"

He smiled and bowed his head some and said, "This is a start."

"What is?"

"Just talking."

I smiled and nodded. "I have a couple of daughters, my youngest is your age."

"Ah, yeah?" he asked.

"If and when you're ready, I think I'd like very much to have a big ol' family dinner. There isn't much that can't be sorted at one of those. Our two families can get a feel for each other and decide if they're either gonna like each other or hate each other." I sighed. "Either way, it'd take some of the uncertainty out of it."

He nodded and laughed a little. "It would at that," he agreed.

"We tend to play games after dinner; ever play that awful card game?"

"The mad-libs one?" he asked.

"That would be the one. We love that game."

He laughed and said, "Well, I'm pretty sure I like the rest of your family already. The fact your son-in-law is a cop I may be able to over-look, depending on if he wins a round or not."

It was my turn to laugh. "More often than not, he's the worst human in the room," I said.

"Game on," he answered with a grin.

"Dinner is every Sunday after church."

He grinned. "We go to church too, just not every Sunday."

I looked at him, amused. "Not even close to the same thing."

"Agree to disagree on that?"

"Fair enough."

"In all honesty, though," he said, his expression sobering. "As awkward as it is for me right now, I have to say, it's good to see my ol' man happy. So, thanks for that."

"I don't really feel like I do anything."

"Well," he said with a gusty sigh, heaving himself up onto his feet as his little boy started to cry for no apparent reason, "whatever it is you aren't doing, keep doing it, because it's working."

He walked down to the water's edge where Everett was picking up their son and he took him from her without hesitation crying, "Hey, Little Man! What's the matter, huh?"

"I don't think he expected the water to be so cold," Everett answered, laughing.

"He wanted to try and walk in it," Dray said and Everett grinned.

"Wait until he hits the terrible twos and he has a full-on meltdown and it takes you ten minutes to figure out it's because you served his milk in the green sippy cup when he wanted the blue one." Shelly smiled, but it held an edge of that mommy-trauma I think every parent knew and loved, at least we loved it looking back on it.

"Oh, Christ. Are you serious?" he asked.

"It's all over the internet, it's called "Why is my kid crying?" and it's *hysterical,* until it happens to you in the middle of the grocery store," the redhead named Mandy said, laughing.

"I'll have to look it up," Dray said, sounding rueful while his boy, in his adorable little alligator swim trunks, quieted against his daddy's shoulder.

I remembered those days fondly, except when it came to Dylan, she went through a phase where she didn't want to have anything to do with Bobby. It'd been heartbreaking, actually. Poor Bobby had just spent too much time on the river as a boat pilot. He'd be gone all week long, get some time off, but poor Dylan. Her young mind just couldn't process all of that. Not when she was still trying to wrap it around learnin' to talk and the like.

"What's that sad look for?" Dragon asked, dropping into the seat on my other side. "Dray say somethin' to you?" His voice was pitched low, like thunder rolling through the clouds with just the barest edge of heat flickering through it like lightning.

I chuckled. "That look was a memory," I said, and told him what I'd been thinkin'. He looked visibly relieved and handed me a red plastic cup with sweet tea in it, loaded with ice.

"I don't think he'd tell you," I murmured as Dray and his family slowly wandered up the beach, "but he's havin' a bit of a struggle gettin' used to things."

"Things?" Dragon asked, the threat of anger evaporating, dissipating into amusement.

I rolled my eyes. "Us. It's new, and he's tryin'," I said, smiling.

"He's a good kid," Dragon said, and pride and affection shaded his tone.

I smiled and said, "Oh, I agree. You've done a fine job raising that young man."

Dragon shook his head, "I don't think I was around enough for that. That was all his mamma's doing."

"I'd like to think it was a team effort," I said kindly, and he smiled and held up his own plastic cup. We clicked them together and I sipped from mine and him from his.

"You good if Blue comes over here and shows you a thing or two?" he asked me after swallowing.

"Yeah, I'm good. Why wouldn't I be good?" I asked.

"You get squirrely any time you're around them."

"I do not!"

"You do, and I didn't say it was a bad thing, it's just something you do." He shrugged nonchalantly and I frowned, unsettled.

"I killed someone dear to them," I said, my voice quiet.

"I know, baby. I know it hurts you, too… but everybody's got to get past it at some point. You can't let grief dictate how you live the rest of your life."

I stared at him, letting my gaze lovingly caress his handsome face and smiled slowly.

"Listen to you, all profound… also, you're kind of one to talk." I winked at him to try and take any sting out of my words, but he felt where I was coming from.

He laughed and nodded and said, "My grief for Tilly took me exactly as long as it needed to so that I could find you."

The way he looked at me as he said it made my throat close up and my eyes grow hot and tight. I was poleaxed, didn't know what to say, frozen in the amber of those honeyed words and the deep sentiment behind them. He reached out and gently tweaked a thumb against my cheek before standing, the spell he had me under lingering even as he walked away, calling over his shoulder, "I'll send Blue over when I see him."

"You do that," I said, my voice echoing hollowly. I was still in shock over his words, which had touched me soul-deep. Then again, Dragon was like that. I don't think anything he did didn't hold meaning. The man was as many-layered as a tree. A rough bark exterior hiding so many golden rings of experience and knowledge. It was a heady and intoxicating mix and I was turning into an alcoholic, unable to get enough of him.

It wasn't long before Blue found me. He asked me quietly, "You have a few minutes?" I smiled up at him and said, "Of course I do," and struggled to get up out of my low seat. He reached down to give me a hand and I had to laugh. Getting comfortable? No problem. Getting up was a whole other story at my age. He smiled at me and led me up to the stone patio under the lodge's great big deck, to a folding table and some of those metal chairs.

"What do you need me for?" I asked.

"Please, sit. I want to show you how we do things."

"Okay," I drawled, a bit nervous.

He smiled at me and pushed a large, square piece of paper in my direction. He set a pen down on top of it and brought out a sheet of his own.

"What am I supposed to do with this?" I asked and he caught my gaze with his.

"You write him a letter," he said. "The idea is to write to those that have gone before, then we fold them into paper boats, put a tea light into the bottom and send them out onto the lake."

"To what end?" I asked solemnly.

"Supposedly, it's a way to speak to them, to tell them the things you couldn't when they were alive, but honestly, I think it's more a way to unburden your own soul. Either way, it's good for you. I mean, at least it has been for me."

"Who reads them?" I asked.

He shook his head. "Nobody. At least, no one alive."

I chewed my bottom lip and he cocked his head, considering me.

"I tell him how much he pissed me off when he was alive," he said quickly and I blinked, taken aback by the vehemence in his tone.

"Really?" I asked in disbelief.

He nodded.

"Just because I loved him, doesn't mean he loved me back. Truth be told, I don't think he was capable. I mean, when he was alive, I thought he did but after…" He trailed off and looked out over the lake, his gaze drifting down to its banks and to Hayley and their son who was playing with the other babies. He swallowed hard.

"Until I was loved by Hayley, I didn't realize that that was how it was supposed to work. Until Cell was gone, I didn't realize just how twisted and fucked-up our relationship was." He turned back towards me and his expression was a mixture of sadness, confusion, and… and I honestly don't know what.

"I'm sorry," I murmured.

"I really wish you weren't," he said. "He did it to himself, it wasn't your fault."

"I know it sounds awful, but I'm beginning to understand that, now. I meant, I'm sorry you feel the way you do. That you're in such a state."

He smiled again and it was genuine. "Don't be, it's getting better, day by day, year by year. Everything happens for a reason. Cell had me blinded, while I don't think I'll ever *not* love him even despite everything he did to me, I realize now that says more about me and who I am than it ever did about him as a person." He gave a rough sigh.

"So, I just write him a letter?" I asked, and Blue nodded.

"That's how it works."

Question was, what do you say to a man you'd never met, except when you killed him? I guess we would find out. I swallowed hard and uncapped the pen.

Dear Cell,

I guess that's what you're called, but I have no idea why. I don't know anything about you, really, and the picture everyone has painted isn't exactly a good one. These are good people you left behind, and I struggle with the fact that I'm both sorry and not for being the one to take you away.

I still feel that way, you know. That it's my fault you're gone. They say you were splitting lanes, and that it's illegal, that you did this to yourself and that it's not my fault, but it sure feels like it is.

Honestly, though. That's enough about me…

I guess, I want you to know that both Blue and Hayley are doing real well despite your absence or perhaps because of it. I guess I'll never really know. I'm told your last words for me were a manipulation; that you were incapable of caring about anyone but yourself. I really don't want to believe that, I mean, the look in your eyes… I guess I have to believe it.

I hope, wherever you're at, you've found a peace that you didn't have when you were alive. I hope, wherever you're at, you can see how well Blue and Hayley are raising your beautiful son.

You can't know how sorry I am that I killed you. I struggle with it every day. I hope wherever you are, you've forgiven me as much as you've found forgiveness. Despite it all, you are much loved and in a lot of ways missed by the people you left behind.

I don't know what else to say, so I'll end this here.

Marcie.

Blue held out a paper towel to me and I took it and wiped my tears and blew my nose. I honestly didn't know what any of this served but hoped that in some way, me putting the words I did to the page helped, as awkward as it was.

"Let me show you how to fold it," he said, and we sat quietly, for several minutes while I followed his careful instruction, fold by fold, to make a beautiful floating paper lantern.

21

D**ragon...**

The memorial had been a bittersweet one, a lot of tears, some smiles, and some finally letting go. It dawned on me why Doc may have wanted to work instead of be there and I'd felt bad about it the entire ride home. I should have asked him, should have called and checked in on him, should have really tried to connect with my best friend...

Woulda, shoulda, coulda... It was hittin' me in the face with all of the force of a sledgehammer as I stood in the doorway of his room.

He could have been asleep, lyin' there flat on his back, one arm at his side, the other folded over his chest, proudly displaying his cut. The fingertips of that hand were touching the smaller Sacred Heart patch on his breast. The other arm had an IV leading into the crook of his arm and I'd seen enough dead men in my time to know.

You didn't get to be that color when you were still breathin', the blood was still flowin'.

"Jesus Christ, Doc…" I murmured, and only snapped-to when I heard one of the women – no, *my* woman – laughing as she came up the hall. I turned but it was too late, she'd seen past me into the room, her blue eyes gone wide. I stopped her, just barely, from yelling out.

"Don't. They don't need to see this." The frozen gears in my mind cracked off their ice coating and started to turn.

"What do we do?" she asked.

I scrapped my bottom lip between my teeth while I calculated things. Cops would investigate, they had to when there was a dead body. That meant they'd take the box of letters sittin' on the bed beside him into evidence, and who knew when or if we'd ever get 'em back.

"I need you to do something for me, for Doc…"

Her brows crushed down into a frown and she was shaking. I doubted she'd ever seen a freshly-dead body in her life and I was sorry she was seeing this, now. I went into the room and returned with the box of letters.

"Dragon, that's illegal!" she hissed when I thrust them into her hands.

"Some things, like this, it ain't about what's *legal*, it's about doin' what's *right*," I declared. "*Please*," I begged her. "Cops get a hold of those, we may never get 'em back, and he wrote them for the people on the envelopes. It ain't law enforcement's business."

Her expression crumbled as she thought about it and she nodded. I kissed her quickly, relief washing through me, and whispered, "Now, go home. Anybody asks you, you had a good weekend, took yourself home, and I called you when you got there with the news. You never saw this, baby."

"Oh, god," she murmured harshly. "You mean I have to get past all those people out there with their friend…" She trailed off and looked past me at Doc, her eyes gathering tears on her lashes like stars and I wanted to break down, myself… but I couldn't. If ever there was a time to toughen up and bootstrap my way through somethin', this was it.

"I'll come by later for the box. Go, baby... please. Go out the back if you have to, the long way around the building."

"Good idea," she murmured, her voice a little hollow as her shellshock set in. "How can you think like that at a time like this?"

I grimaced on the inside but kept my face stone on the outside as I thought one word: *practice.*

Outwardly, I ignored her question and turned her gently towards the back door.

"I'll call you as soon as I can," I murmured.

"Okay, and, ...Dragon?" She turned, and her eyes were so sincere, so pain-filled on my behalf when she said, "I'm so sorry about your friend..."

It bent me damn near to breaking, but I wouldn't and couldn't break. Not with the whole of the club out there depending on me holding my shit together.

She disappeared out the back door and I squared my shoulders and pulled out my phone. I called my Vice President.

"Pops, what're you callin' me for?" he answered, laughing.

"Grab Data and Trig. Meet me by Doc's room," I ordered.

The laughter died and my Vice President replaced my boy in half a heartbeat.

"On our way."

The phone went dead in my ear and I took a second and leaned heavily on the doorjamb leading into Doc's room, staring at my friend, a war of emotions going on inside, that most? Most, I didn't even have names for.

It was gonna be a long night.

∽

"IT'S NOT UNUSUAL," the deputy said, his little notepad in his hand, pen poised over the paper, even though he wasn't looking at it, he was lookin' at me. "Less than half of all suicides leave a note."

I nodded and put my hands on my hips, bowing my head and trying not to smack the shit out of this kid. He was speakin' so nonchalantly, like it weren't my best fuckin' friend bein' zipped into a fuckin' body bag just feet in front of me.

"How long until we can have him back?"

"You've been through this before, I reckon," the deputy said and I gritted my teeth.

"Can't say that I have," I said coldly.

"Hey, Dad," Dray called and I looked over. I gave a nod and said, "Excuse me," and moved that way. Trigger smoothly taking my place in front of the deputy. He was better at dealing with a LEO's bullshit, especially when it came to somethin' strikin' such a nerve in me.

I leaned against the wall facin' my son and his dark eyes that so mirrored my own searched my face. His jaw tightened and he gave a nod, his hand coming up and gripping the sleeve of my jacket at my shoulder and I took the silent strength he offered because I wasn't doin' good. I wasn't okay. I was shook, hardcore, right to my core. I was angry, at Doc, at myself, at the Deputy, at the universe for dealing us such a shit hand...

Did it really? That voice of self-doubt reared up, followed quickly by its kissing cousin, derision... *Or is this just Karma back to bite you?*

It was weighing on me heavy as they wheeled Doc out the back door to the medical examiner's rig waiting on the track.

"You good to address our people, or you want I should do it?" Dray asked, his expression as grim as mine as we watched them load him into the back of the nondescript Ford Econoline van.

"What kind of leader would I be to leave my people to suffer in the face of my own?" I asked him.

And without missing, a beat my boy answered.

"A human one, who just lost his best friend."

I cracked then, tears welling up hot and fierce, and for the first time in a long time, I eased part of my burden down. I looked back at my boy and asked, "Can you talk to 'em, please?"

"Yeah, Pops. Come on, let's go."

22

Marcie...

I heard him roll up, the gravel crunching beneath his bike's tires, his engine revving and chugging as he'd worked his way up the driveway. He sat, letting his bike idle as I watched him through the kitchen window. He looked some kind of broken, sitting there astride his motorcycle, his hands resting on the tank, his shoulders hunched. I could see his heart was fractured and aching and an echoing fractured ache went out from mine to his in a silent plea for him to come into the house.

It was one he must have heard, since he heeled down the stand and leaned his bike over onto it. He got up with the weight of the world on his leather-clad shoulders and I opened the door before one of his booted feet could even touch the bottom step. He looked up sharply, his eyes narrowing, and I leaned against the doorframe and held a hand out to him. He took the two steps up and reached out and took it, and I almost reeled him in the rest of the way.

It was like he needed my touch, my help, to traverse those final steps to reach what was sitting at my little kitchen table. He stopped just inside the door and stared at it for a long time, a mix of emotions crossing his face, flickering through those coal-dark eyes and I knew the fire that was eating him up from the inside. I drew him carefully into the house, further, where he dropped like a stone into the chair that was pulled out. He stared at that wooden box, envelopes with names leaning against the back, sticking over the top, and he leaned forward, his eyes fixed on it. He braced his leather-clad forearms on his knees, bowed his head and the dam broke.

He wept, and it was all I could do to be the rock he needed as he was battered by the storm.

I scrambled forward, kneeling on my kitchen floor in front of him, and put my arms around him. His arms went around me as he leaned heavily, brokenly, against me and sobbed, these great, broken, heaving sobs that wracked his whole body and shook us both. I felt my own tears spring to my eyes as I hurt for him and I held him tight and lied to him.

"It's alright, it's all right now, you just let it out, I'm right here. I've got you, baby. I won't let you fall."

I lied, because it wasn't all right, it wasn't okay, and this poor man… hadn't he already lost so much?

He held onto me as if I were the last thing left to him and I held onto him as tightly as I could as if to say, *I'm here, I'm not going anywhere any time soon…* because what else could I do?

WE SAT AT THE TABLE, side by side, two steaming mugs of coffee cooling in front of us, the box with its contents sitting just beyond our drinks looking almost expectant. There were two envelopes out of the mess, one in front of Dragon, and one, complete with my name on it, in front of me…

Of course, he'd spelled Marcie wrong, the cursive script which was almost way too nice for a doctor spelling it M-A-R-C-Y, but then again we hadn't known each other at all. We'd only just met, the one time, two days ago. It made me wonder what he could possibly have to say to me. I lifted my gaze from that unremarkable cream envelope and looked at Dragon who was staring at his.

"I should probably get back to the club," he said.

"They waitin' for you?" I asked.

He shook his head. "Naw, they've all gone home."

I frowned. "Then why go back, if no one's waitin' for you? Why on earth spend the night alone in that awfully big place, all by yourself just after something like this? No," I shook my head. "I won't have it. You're stayin' right here with me."

"I couldn't impose..." he said with a sad smile, and I shook my head harder.

"You ain't, and I won't hear nothin' of it. You're here now, with me, and it's gonna stay that way, so you might as well get comfortable."

"Jesus, you're bossy, woman."

"You're damn right I am," I said and took a resolute sip of my coffee. Of course, I couldn't make him stay if he didn't want to, so here was to hopin' the man would see sense and that he would stay.

"All right, all right, calm your tits. I'll stay with you, Sugar. Truth be told, I think I need to. Only..."

I raised an eyebrow. "Only?"

"You got anything stronger 'n coffee?"

"Like?"

"Tequila would be welcome."

"I think I got a bottle in the back of my liquor cabinet. Can't promise it's any good, though. No idea what brand it is. I don't drink the stuff."

"Right now, I don't much care, Sugar. I just want to lean on my old friend to deal with the loss of my best one."

His words made fresh tears spring to my eyes and I sniffed, cleared my throat, and stood up saying, "I'll see what I can come up with."

I went into the liquor cabinet in the dining room and came back with the unopened, lone bottle of tequila from the back. I didn't even know where it came from. I set it on the table beside Dragon and set a bottle of my favorite Kentucky bourbon beside my coffee mug. I went for a glass for him, because unlike bourbon, I didn't think tequila went good in coffee.

When I turned around, he had the bottle out in front of him, peering through his readers at it.

"This ain't bad stuff, you sure you want to open it?"

"I'm sure. If ever there was an occasion..." I set the glass by his hand and he nodded.

"If ever there were, at that," he agreed.

I uncapped my bottle and added a splash of bourbon to my coffee. Meanwhile, Dragon poured a healthy measure of tequila into the glass I'd brought him. He looked at it, sighed, and said, "This is a damn shame," and downed the contents of his first pour.

I couldn't tell if he meant about his friend or the alcohol, and it didn't really seem appropriate to ask, so I didn't. I sat back in my seat and he patted the top of his chaps-clad knee. I put my feet up and crossed them at the ankle. He smoothed a warm, rough hand along my skin, the top of my foot, along the top of my ankle, as high as he could go along my shin before my jeans stopped him, and back down. Back and forth, touching me as if I was his worry stone, and maybe, right now, I was.

"Talk to me, love," I murmured.

He tipped his head back and let out a gusty sigh, staring at my kitchen ceiling as the daylight began to die. He shook his head gently, sniffed back more tears and cleared his throat.

"I wasn't always good to Doc," he said, finally. "He came to the club by way of a real bad gambling addiction. One I enabled, to a point, to get him in our debt in case we needed medical care off the books. It was all business at first, but Doc... Doc surprised me."

I smiled and I knew it held an edge of sadness, when I really meant for it to be encouraging.

He told me all about his and Doc's long history. It was an amazing story made better when Doc met Chandra. Chandra's tragic end made my heart ache for Doc and the rest of the club, and put certain things in perspective.

"Sounds like Doc's been hurtin' for a real long time," I murmured.

Dragon nodded and wiped his eyes, "I'm so pissed one minute, but it's like I can't stay angry the next, you know? Doc never had any kids of his own, Chandra's kids turned their back when she died. After my Tilly... I had Dray, the club, I had *Doc* to hold me together, and I'm tellin' you, babe, I feel like I failed him."

I shook my head, "I don't think so, honey. I think he was just hurting... Then again, he's left letters to all of you, which tells me he loved you all so very much. Maybe it's a bit early to open that up and read it, but..."

"No, you're right. I should," he said, and picked up his readers from off the table.

"Would you like a little privacy?" I asked quietly.

He nodded. "For this? Yeah."

"Go on in the living room, use the reading lamp and my chair." I picked up my letter and stood, bending and kissing him softly. "When you're ready, you come on to bed."

He nodded and sniffed and poured himself some more tequila, capping the bottle. I went down the hall and I heard him click on the lamp in the living room. I set my letter on the nightstand and turned on the lamp in my bedroom. I made sure I had a pair of reading glasses in here and set about getting ready for bed myself. That done, and with nothing left to do, I piled pillows behind my back, sat myself up with the blankets in my lap, and plucked the expensive-feeling envelope off of the night table.

He'd sealed the cream paper with crimson wax, the club's Sacred Heart raised in the wax. He'd taken time and care with each one of these, and it was time to find out what he had to say to me.

I carefully lifted the wax seal and let out a breath I'd been holding. It was so pretty, I hadn't wanted to crack it, or break it. I slipped my glasses onto my face and slid the single sheet of thick, matching cream paper out of the sturdy envelope.

Dear Marcy,

I'm sure you're wondering 'what the hell' and I'm real sorry about ruining your weekend, but after seeing you and him at the fire last night… well, I knew it was time. I knew my boy D. had found someone to take care of him and watch his ass, and that I could go.

I just wanted to say thank you for being that person for him. Thank you, and honestly, woman, no hard feelings about Cell. You didn't do anything wrong and you need to stop carrying that guilt around. I know I don't have the right to ask, but if you could do me a favor and make sure Dragon doesn't carry any guilt around about me, I'd be mighty grateful. I wish I could have gotten to know you better, but I feel like I got a pretty solid feel for you.

You're a good woman, and Dragon's a good man.

I miss my woman. Life ain't the same without her, and it's just not a life worth living any more. I'm sure Dragon will let you know all about it, but as of now, I'm about all wrote out. You're my last letter, but probably the most important.

Look after him for me, since I can't be there.

All the love I got left,

Doc

I lowered the letter to my lap, tears streaming down my face at the unfairness of it all. I set it, and my glasses, aside on the table and slid down in my bed. I lay there, alone, thinking, and hoping that Dragon would come to bed soon.

23

Dragon…

I sat in the chair Marcie had indicated and had pulled the cord on the stained glass lamp above my head. I set the glass of tequila aside after one more fortifying sip and sighed, heavy and broken. I swallowed hard and raised the envelope, stained with my name on its front in Doc's spider-silk cursive.

I closed my eyes, and lowered the paper back to my lap, the leather of my jacket and cut creaking in the intimate golden pool of light from my lady's lamp and somehow, sitting here, knowing she was just in the other room, knowing that she'd offered me her safe space, the one she spent the most time in, reading her books… Well, I took strength from all of it. The kind of strength that only the love of a good woman could provide. I put my glasses on my face, sucked it the fuck up, and cracked the seal on the envelope of thick paper.

DON'T BE PISSED…

Hell, I know you're pissed, but knowing you, you're feeling guilty as hell, too. Don't. This decision has been a long time comin' and it ain't just about Chandra, either. This is me, goin' out on my own terms, D.

I'm sick.

I know y'all have been makin' comments about me losin' weight and shit, and you aren't wrong, but it wasn't just about my girl. It's my prostate. It's also too far gone for me to do anything about it. So just, don't. This ain't you. It was never about you, or anyone else but me.

I know we didn't get the best start, but that was because the best was yet to come. You did more for me than I could ever thank you for. You gave me purpose again. You gave me a new, healthier kind of rush to pursue so I could leave the cards and the dice behind. You gave me Chandra, by facilitating us meeting, and she was the best thing to ever happen to me, D. Hands down. She was and always will be the love of my life to the very end.

If anyone should feel guilty it's me, man. I didn't know. I couldn't know what losing the other half of your soul felt like until I lost her, and yet there I was, makin' you live through it day in, day out, for years after you lost Tilly.

I've been carrying guilt over that since Chandra died, but you... you never once said 'I told you so' or even brought it up. You helped me deal with it, the same, if not better than I had hoped I helped you, which is why I need you to know this ain't your fault. None of it.

God, or whatever powers that be, just saw fit that it was time for me to go. Sure, I could have done the chemo, been sick, pissin' myself and a bunch of other unpleasant side effects to buy me a few more months, but that ain't the way we lived. We don't follow the rules and regulations of the citizen normative - or whatever the fuck fancy-ass name you want to put on it.

That ain't us. That ain't me since you showed me there was a better way of doin' things. I've had the best life since meeting you. I couldn't ask for anything better out of my life with Chandra, either. There ain't enough thanks in the world for me to give you for being my friend, for introducing me to her.

I feel like I am dealing you a real shit hand by going out this way, and I'd be lying if I said I wasn't scared... but I figure this is the best way. A kindness to not only myself, but to everyone. I don't want to waste away and I don't want none of you to be burdened with watching it.

Fuck, I'm rambling, ain't I? I didn't want to do that.

I love you, my brother, my best friend. I'll be waitin' for you with a bottle of your favorite tequila, for as long as it takes, but take your fuckin' time.

I'm a whole lot less worried about leaving now that I've seen you with Marcy. You're a lucky son of a bitch, you know that?

Of course you know that.

There's some things in an envelope in the safe in my closet. I want my bike to go to Disney. That boy needs to know what a Harley feels like instead of that princess, prima donna, German piece of shit he's been puttering around tryin' to keep up with the rest of us on. Let his ol' man ride that shit. So, the title to my bike is in there and already signed over to him.

I really want you to take care of Chandra's books. I can't bear to donate them, and I know it's stupid, but even after I'm gone, I want a part of her there, too. She loved all of you all only second best to me. Don't let them leave the club.

My shit from 'Nam, the medals and the military paperwork and shit, also in the safe, make sure it goes to Trigger. I think he'd have the right kind of reverence for it. My guns, I've signed over to Ghost...

I skimmed over all of the shit he was doling out to everyone. It was just stuff. I didn't care about any of it, but I would see that his wishes were tended. I pulled my glasses off and ran a hand over my face, thinkin' to myself, *Fuck, Doc... why didn't you tell me?*

Not surprising, he had somethin' to say about that after the division of all the rest of his worldly fuckin' goods...

I didn't tell any of you about being sick because I know you would have talked me into fighting it, and I would have, because I love you all... I just wasn't that brave, and I hope y'all will forgive me for that someday.

Until we meet again, my brother. Take care of you, take care of Marcy, and let the club hold you up where I let you down.

I really mean it, I love you all and I miss you already.

Sacred Hearts Forever – Forever Sacred Hearts,

Doc.

P.S. – For what it's worth, I would have voted Dray in as President when the time came. Not because I know it's what you want, but because he's the right man for the job. He's learned so much and you done good – yes, you. Just give him a year or two more. That boy's aging into a fine man. Oh, and quit smokin'. See you on the other side. Hopefully not soon.

I tossed the letter aside on the little table between the two armchairs and sniffed. I tossed my readers aside and picked up the tequila, taking a fortifying drink. I needed a cigarette. I got up, taking my glass with me and opened up Marcie's back door. The night was cool, but not cold, and the house felt a little stuffy from sittin' closed up and empty all weekend, so I left the door open. I went over and sat sideways on my bike, bracing my boots in the gravel.

Tequila glass on my bitch seat, safe from tippin', I fished out a cigarette from the pack and put it between my lips. I heaved a sigh and found my lighter, lit up the cancer stick and sucked in a lungful of tobacco smoke. I tipped my head all the way back and stared up into the star-scattered sky and wondered which one was Doc lookin' down over us, because I knew he had to be up there. There weren't no finer man in this life or the next.

"Take care of him, girls…" I murmured, and sighed. The only thing I had goin' for me is that I knew he was there with Chandra and Tilly now, and I could totally count on 'em all to take care of each other. It's what we did.

"Sacred Hearts forever, forever Sacred Hearts," I murmured, and downed the rest of what was in my glass.

24

Marcie…

I heard him go out and I panicked slightly, thinkin' he was tryin' to leave after all that drinkin'. I threw back the blankets on my bed and padded carefully around it to my bedroom window and peeked out into the back. He was leanin' that nice butt of his against the saddle of his bike, but he weren't goin' nowhere.

Instead, he set his drink aside and pulled out one of those damn cigarettes. I let out a breath I hadn't realized I'd been holding in relief. Not going anywhere, just indulging in his bad habit. I could live with that. I watched him take that first lungful of smoke. He held it, tipping his head all the way back and stared for a long time into the sky. I saw him murmur something to the stars and my heart broke all over again.

I backed away from the window slowly, suddenly feeling like I was intruding, and crept back into bed. I lay on my side and closed my eyes, tears leaking out from under my closed lids and tickling over my skin, dripping down my nose.

"Oh, tarnation!" I muttered and wiped at them with the back of my hand, impatiently. I sighed and tried to settle into sleep, and I must have drifted off some, because when I woke, it was to the bed dipping behind me as Dragon sat on the edge of it.

I breathed in the smell of alcohol, the outdoors, and cigarette smoke clinging to him. The first two weren't so bad, but the last I could always do without. He rested a hand on my hip and rubbed it through the comforter and I twisted so I could look at him. He lifted the blankets and got into bed with me, pulling me back against his chest.

I snuggled into him and he said, "I don't know how to feel anymore, I'm just kind of numb."

"Yer emotionally and mentally exhausted, honey. It's to be expected, it's human," I said simply. He nodded and held me tight, pressing a kiss to the back of my shoulder.

"Feel like talkin'?" I asked.

"Yes and no," he answered.

"Anything I can do?" I asked when he was silent for too long.

"I honestly don't know, baby."

I turned onto my back and he put his arms around me, pressing his ear to the center of my chest between my breasts. He sighed out softly, and his body eased, losing some of the tension it held. I smiled faintly as he listened to the ticking of my heartbeat and I played with his hair, gently stroking my fingers through it until, I think, we both fell asleep.

I WOKE ALL ALONE the next morning and when I peeked out my bedroom window, I was relieved to see his bike was still here. I found him sitting at the kitchen table in front of a steaming mug of coffee, staring sightlessly at the box of letters.

"Y' all right?" I asked gently from the kitchen archway and he startled sharply, his hand going reflexively under his jacket. I froze and he froze, too, when he registered it was only me.

"Bad idea sneakin' up on me, Sugar."

"Honestly, with how hard you were thinkin', I don't think anything short of me bringin' a marchin' band through the house would get any other kind of reaction."

He chuckled and said, "I probably woulda shot the tuba player. Y' okay?"

"Oh, I'll be fine," I said, moving into the kitchen. "Soon as my heart crawls its way back down into my chest where it belongs."

"Sorry," he said gruffly and I inclined my head gently.

I brought a fresh mug down out of the cupboard.

"All's forgiven, no worries."

The ensuing silence was so loud it very nearly echoed through my kitchen. The atmosphere so very heavy with his thoughts as I poured myself some coffee and joined him at the table. I sat down and doctored it up, leaving out the bourbon this time, and after my first sip, I asked gently, "What's on your mind?"

He sighed, a heavy, frustrated thing and said, "So much. I ain't hardly know where to begin."

"All you gotta do is pick one, baby. Just one little thing, or maybe the biggest. Just one thing, and all the rest'll follow."

"Hm." He sucked in a long breath and said, "I'm tired, Sugar. So very tired."

"Of what?"

"Being the man."

I raised my eyebrows and he chuckled and shook his head. "Not that man, the man in charge." He cast his gaze back onto the line of letters in the box and sighed again. "I don't want to be the man to hand these out," he said finally.

"Then don't," I said. "Let someone else do it."

He gave me a look like that would happen when Hell froze over and the little devils went shopping. I took another drink of my coffee and gave him questioning eyes over the rim of my cup.

"That's not how it goes, baby."

"I thought you made your own rules."

"I do, and this is one of 'em. I don't ask anything of anyone that I'm not willin' to do myself."

"It's a noble rule."

He sighed, a heavy thing, and nodded. "Sometimes I wish I could break it."

"I know, but if y' did, would you ever be able to forgive yourself?"

He chuckled and shook his head.

"When did you get to know me so well?"

I smiled and said, "Sometimes, it's like lookin' into a mirror when it comes to our beliefs."

"Hey, now," he said, gravely. "That sounds an awful lot like you're sayin' I'm some kind of a good man."

"Aren't you?" I asked innocently.

"Now that, I ain't," he said with such a heartbreaking certainty.

"We'll have to agree to disagree on that," I said quietly.

He reached out and cupped my cheek and my eyes darted to his face which had such a look of appreciation on it, it gave me real pause. How many times had I wished a man would look at me like that? Too many to count. I put my hand over his and turned my lips into his palm and we just sat there, quietly, our other hands twined on the top of my thigh until, with another heavy sigh, he said, "I better rally the troops back at base."

"You want I should go with you?" I asked.

He shook his head. "You've got clients, ain't you?"

I nodded. "But I could cancel."

"No, don't do that. Just call me when you're done for the day, yeah?"

"I can do that," I agreed.

"Thanks."

25

Dragon…

It ripped me to pieces handing out those letters. The looks on all of their faces. Grim. Ashen. Eyes red-rimmed from weeping, shoulders hunched as if it was the only thing holding some of them together. Some tore into their envelopes right away, some stared at the fancy thick paper in their hands, some tucked them into the inside pockets of their cuts for later.

Disney read his and his reaction was probably the most shocking, the most out-of-character of all. He stood up abruptly, sucking in a sharp breath, and launched the chair he'd been sitting in into the cinderblock wall. It shattered in a clatter of splinters and he dropped to the cement floor, rocking and weeping. His ol' man, Aaron, went to him, and Sunshine did too. They held him between them while he wailed and cried, screaming his agony wordlessly, trying like hell to get rid of that overpowering, overwhelming pain.

It damn-near broke me to watch it, but as much as I wanted to, I couldn't join him on that floor.

I had to be strong, resilient for all of 'em. I needed to hold them up, and fuck if I weren't so fuckin' *tired* of always being the one.

"You okay, Pops?"

I startled. I thought my boy had gone home with all the rest. I downed what was in my glass and shook my head.

"I'm really not, boy. I'm really not," I said and I could feel myself tremble as I held myself in. My boy, to his credit, dropped down onto the stool beside mine and slapped me on the back of my cut, put an arm around me and just sat there, silently lending me the strength I needed to get my shit together.

"I can do it, Pops. Whatever you need me to do, just lay it on me."

It was a small thing, but a profound one. I was so proud of the man my boy had become in that moment, I damn-near teared up for a completely different reason. I supposed now was as good a time as any to start passing the torch like I intended and I sighed.

"I need to show you how to go about doing things in the event of a member's death. Where the papers are for the cemetery plots. Who to contact, how to arrange things. I guess now is as good a time as any."

He nodded. "I'm ready when you are."

I nodded and said, "Come on with me."

SOME HOURS LATER, I leaned back in my desk chair in the converted janitor's closet that served as my office. Dray sat in a metal folding chair in the doorway, shaking his head.

"Never realized how much shit went into planning a funeral."

"It's a lot," I agreed.

He shook his head. "Hope I never have to cause to put this particular knowledge to use."

"You will. At least one more time."

"Don't talk like that, Pops," he almost scolded me.

"Not anytime soon, you dumbass," I rocked forward in my chair and sighed. "Guess I could have worded it better."

"You think?" he asked, standing and stretching. He folded up the chair and tucked it back behind the filing cabinet it came from. He let his eyes wander over the pictures on the walls of a bygone era. Photos of me with Unkind and Doc, Tilly tucked into my side as we stood in front of the bikes and the old clubhouse.

"I don't miss that place," he said frankly, and I had to laugh a little.

"Place was a shithole, for sure. Glad we scored this one on the cheap."

"What'd you have on the real estate agent?" he asked, eyes still locked on one of the photos with a much younger Doc in it.

"Should get that one blown up for the memorial," I said, ignoring his question.

He shook his head, "I got one already. One of him and Chandra at the last Lake Run they managed to do together before she died."

I nodded. "That's even better," I agreed.

"Want I should take care of that now?"

I nodded, "Yeah, if you wouldn't mind. Need to start getting this place set up."

"You good?"

I nodded again, and said, "As good as it gets, given the circumstances."

"All right."

He punched the door frame twice, lightly, and left. I watched him go, the ends of his dark hair, so like my own, brushing the top of his top rocker. It'd been getting longer. I hadn't noticed. I sighed, heavy and leaned way back in my seat, letting my gaze rove over the old photographs on the walls, reminiscing about the good ol' times until my eyes started to water unbidden and I had to cast my eyes to the water-stained tiles of the ceiling.

"Wherever y' are, whatever yer doing, I hope you're happy, and everything's good," I muttered and picked up my glass. It was fuckin' broken, and by broken, I meant empty. That was all right. I was done in here anyhow.

I heaved myself to my feet and went back out to the bar and poured myself another. My phone buzzed in my hand but I didn't have my glasses on; I'd left 'em back on my desk, so rather than try and read the screen, I just answered.

"Yeah."

"Yeah? Is that any way to answer the phone?" Marcie asked through the line. I could hear the smile in her voice which took any real admonition or nagging out of the quip.

I smiled myself and said, "Left my damn glasses on my desk. Just finished up with Doc's arrangements, insofar that I could make 'em."

"Oh, I'm sorry..." her whole demeanor changed and I could feel her hurt for me through the miles separating us and it did my heart some good, strangely enough.

"I'll be okay," I murmured, but I didn't feel it.

She sighed and asked, "You coming over for dinner?"

"Mm, can't," I said, taking a sip from my glass.

"Why not?"

"Been drinkin', ain't safe to ride."

Silence, then after a span of heartbeats, "I'm on my way over."

She hung up before I could say anything and I had to smile looking at the screen as it flashed the call ended signal. Albeit, blurry as fuck. I got back up and downed the rest of my tequila I'd poured and swore off any more for the night. I had a little stronger than a buzz going, and I think it was safe to say I was over the line into drunk.

I went back to my office and retrieved my glasses, and locking up behind me, went to Data's fishbowl.

Weren't nobody at the club and I couldn't say I blamed any of 'em. If I had my way, I'd take a bit of a break from it, too, just a night or two, but I didn't. I lived here full time, this big ol' place all to myself since Red and Dani finished fixing up his cabin to live in.

I was okay with that. This place was still everyone's central hub, and it felt good knowing everyone had somebody, had loves, jobs, had lives outside this place to some extent, but still made room to make this club and the family it represented central to their beings despite it all. I stared at the camera for the front gate and waited on Marcie's car to show on the feed and smiled to myself.

The club that I built, and everyone in it, was thriving and I couldn't ask for a better fit for the misfits that called it home. It was everything it was supposed to be and more, and I think Doc had seen that. He knew we would get through it; that we'd be good, and I couldn't say I wouldn't have gone the same route, if it were me in his place.

Headlights flashed on the screen and I hit the keystrokes to open the gate, the iron rolling aside to let her in, up the drive. She parked on the next screen over, right in front of the doors and I got up to go meet my lady-love and take some of my own solace, the way the rest of my crew was.

26

Marcie...

He'd met me at the door, assured me we were the only ones here and kissed me hard, the taste of tequila and pain strong, almost overwhelming. We'd fucked against the bar, then wound up in his room, and forgot about dinner for the time being. I lay listening to his heartbeat, my ear over the ink under his skin depicting the true-to-life drawing of the SHMC's Sacred Heart over where his real one resided.

He toyed with my skin, fingertips trailing passionately along it while his mind was a million miles away. Where it'd gone, I couldn't tell you. He just stared blankly into the dark, eyes unfocused, expression unreadable from what I could make of it, and I couldn't help but sigh.

"What're you thinkin'?" I asked softly.

"Wasn't really," he said, sucking in a breath.

I pushed myself up and straddled his hips, writhing slightly against his soft cock, and smiled when it immediately began to stir back to life.

"Thought you was satisfied," he said with a smirk.

"Never," I murmured and bent to kiss him. He held my face to his gently and worked his hips, his body sliding against mine, working for purchase naturally, unassisted. I wiggled, he thrust and we fit together like two pieces of a puzzle, his dick sliding into my hot, wet heat slowly.

I groaned against his lips as he seated himself all the way inside my body and thrust just that little bit more, in that way that drove me wild. I pushed up off his shoulders, tearing my mouth from his and he let me, his hands drifting to my hips to encourage me to ride him, and ride him I did. Slow, easy movements of my hips, lifting myself on knees and slipping back down his shaft, grinding deliciously when our bodies met. He smiled, this charmed little half-smile and watched me move and the look in his eyes... well, it made me feel worshipped, like I was some kind of goddess made flesh.

I rolled my hips and his eyes fluttered shut, and it was like the moan that slipped from my lips was the sweetest music he ever heard. We made love in perfect synchronicity and it left me wondering where he'd been all my life.

"God, yeah, Sugar. Fuck me. Fuck me just like that," he whispered, his voice strained, and I loved how he talked dirty to me. He had this way about him, talkin' dirty, sure, but makin' me feel like some kind of princess just the same. He talked dirty, but he never made me feel dirty. If anything, he made sure I felt every inch of him inside me as we wallowed in the mud *together*. Sex with Dragon was never one-sided, was always a joyous occasion, no matter how heavy things from the outside got.

His hands traveled over my skin, smoothing up my ribs to cup and knead my breasts while I ground our bodies together. His eyes were heavy-lidded with lust, both of us breathing heavy in the close dark. Eventually, it was like he couldn't stand it anymore and he took one hand away, placing his thumb between us over my clit, teasing it to life. My pussy spasmed around his cock and I threw back my head and gasped.

"Oh, yeah. That's it, come for me, darlin'."

I tried to resist, tried to drag it out longer, my body spiraling higher, tighter around him, gripping him like a clenched fist until he grunted and that grunt seemed to be all I needed. I cried out, and he made good on his promise from the lake – he was there to catch me as I fell as if from a great height, greater than even the stars in the sky. It was like he sent me to heaven but I couldn't stay.

Unfortunately, with everything going on down here, I wish it didn't feel like I was crashing right back down into a certain type of Hell.

I thought, somewhat selfishly to myself, *Of all the times and ways to die, why did you have to pick now and why did it have to be like that, mister?*

I was lying on top of my lover, panting and out of breath, and I jolted when he answered me, "Because that's how it is when it comes to our folk, and that's how we roll."

I pushed myself up, crimson with embarrassment.

"I didn't mean to say that out loud," I stammered.

"It's all right." He reached up and grazed a thumb against my cheek in a light touch.

"You ain't gotta keep secrets from me, Marcie. Never, for anything, my feelings don't bruise that easy and I like that you have questions – that you *want* to know how we roll."

"I want to understand," I murmured. "But I can't promise that I always will…"

"You won't always," he said and sat up abruptly, putting his arms around me, sitting me up in his lap, his cock driving deeper even as it started to go limp, touching off little aftershocks inside me. I shuddered and he grinned and wiggled a little to get me going again.

I smacked his shoulder and cried, "Would you stop! We're havin' a moment here!"

He chuckled and it was a genuine sound as he said, "Is that what we're doin' now?"

"Yes, damn it! I mean, isn't it?"

He rested his chin on my chest between my breasts and looked up at me with such... I don't know, but whatever it was, I liked it.

"You're so behind on the curve, but you're quick, baby. I'll give you that." He sighed and it sounded worried. "This life ain't for everybody, though, and I'm afraid eventually, something will be too much... it's already pretty heavy around here."

I felt a strange sort of tension ease out of my shoulders and told him the truth, "You're right, something might come along that'll be too much, even for me... and when it does, we'll deal with it." I put all the iron determination behind my voice that I could manage.

"Yeah?" he asked, that halfcharmed smile back on his lips.

"Yes," I said. "I may be just another citizen to y'all, but at the same time, I don't think I am. I got something the rest of them don't," I said.

"You do," he agreed. I raised my eyebrows.

"An' just what do you think that is?" I asked.

He pressed a kiss between my breasts and huffed a sigh. "An open mind, for one. An open heart for another. You got a willingness to learn, an' adapt. If you didn't, I wouldn't have started any of this with you."

"Why did you?" I asked in a curious whisper, and his arms twined around me, and it was as if he were trying to lend some of his physical strength to me emotionally in this moment because in this moment, I think I was as vulnerable as I ever let myself be with a man... with anybody.

"Because, you've got a fire inside. You're compassionate, you're strong, and you've got everything to you that I think I been missin', that I think I need."

I traced fingertips along his lips and frowned slightly, "You have all of those things," I said, confused.

"Had... I *had* all of those things. Since I lost 'em, I ain't been nothin' but a pale imitation fakin' it 'til I make it. With you at my side, I ain't fakin' it anymore."

I sat in his lap, silent, motionless, awestruck at his words. I swallowed hard, and fought back the tears that threatened. He smiled up at me and drew me down into another lingering kiss and if I had any doubts, any at all, that this man truly held love for me, they were scattered to the four winds.

All I could think to say was, "Well, I love you, too."

He laughed, a deep one from his belly and asked, "You hungry? 'Cause I'm starvin'."

"Hell, yes," I answered. "Dinnertime was hours ago."

"C'mon, I'll treat you to the finest fuckin' pizza delivery can provide."

I gave a dubious laugh, "Right, some high-class joints come all the way out here." I rolled my eyes.

"Only the best for you, babe."

I smiled and for a moment, the heartbreak of the last few days was left off to the side.

~

"So what's to expect?" I asked, setting down my unwanted crust.

He finished chewing and said, "Lot of hard partying, drinkin', smokin', fuckin', you name it."

"A party?" I asked, my tone a mixture of disbelief and surprise.

"Yup, biker funerals ain't like citizen funerals. We mourn in our own ways, leading up to the wake, but once it's here, it's a celebration of Doc's life in the truest sense of the words."

I gave a slightly impressed look as I mulled over what he was telling me.

"So, like, what do you do?"

He chuckled and wiped pizza grease off his mouth with a napkin and said, "Doc loved to gamble, so I'm guessin' there will be cards, and bettin' on pool. He was a gamblin' addict before the club, managed to kick the habit and keep it to just recreational with the boys after that. We didn't play for money on account of his addiction."

I wrinkled my brow, "So what did you play for then? Just chips?"

He gave a feral grin. "Chores around the club when we didn't have prospects to do 'em. Shit jobs on runs, that kind of thing."

"High stakes, just not money, then," I said, grinning.

"Damn right, no one wanted to dig and maintain the latrine. Doc ended up doin' it more 'n his fair share. He was crap at keepin' a poker face."

I laughed and said, "I been known to hold my own at a hand of poker."

"Oh, yeah? Gonna have to put that to the test with some strip poker."

I laughed. "No, thank you!"

"Thought you wanted to try new things," he said with a wink.

"With you! Not the rest of the club, not just yet. Good Lord, ain't a single one of 'em gonna wanna see that."

"Hey, now," he said, and caught my eye with his. "You might be surprised."

I rubbed my lips together and tried to decide if he was joking or not, I finally had to decide on 'not.'

"Y'all are different," I said, finally. "I'll give you that."

Dragon grinned and took it for the compliment I meant it to be and I was relieved, he could have taken it to mean any number of things. I was glad we were growing to know one another that way.

"So when does this all happen?" I asked.

"Soon as they release Doc's body, he'll go to the funeral home, they'll bring him here, we'll have our night of fun; and then hung over as fuck the next morning, we ride. Take him home to his final resting place with the rest of our boys that have gone before."

I took a deep breath and let it out slow, "So, in the meantime, what can *I* do?"

He smiled, "You're doin' it," he said and covered my hand with his own where it rested on the table. "You're here, ain't yah?"

I cocked my head and looked at him.

"I'll always be here, too. I think you can count on that."

He nodded and kissed my hand, and that was all that needed to be said about it, honestly.

27

D ragon...

The wake went off about as expected. Drunk, loud, rowdy, with a fuck-ton of gambling and fucking. Doc would have been proud, but holy fuck my head was pounding the next morning, and by morning, I meant noon. We all hauled ass out of bed, heads throbbing like a cannon went off between our ears, slogging out into the common room for a last visit with Doc, who looked like he might as well be asleep.

That fucked with me. The makeup job the mortuary did was almost too fuckin' good. I stopped by his open, glossy black casket, lined in white satin, the handles and clasps, the accent pieces all gleaming silver, and leaned a hip against it. I sniffed and cleared my throat and lit up a cigarette.

"I'm gonna miss you, you son of a bitch," I muttered and sighed.

"Wish you'd just fuckin' *told* me. You know I would have played it close to my cut, would have done whatever you wanted done. You didn't trust me, you didn't have to go alone like that. I could have been there for you."

I sighed and put a hand on the coffin lid and took one last look at my best friend layin' there in his cut, poker chips and photographs surrounding him, some flowers from my late wife's garden in there, too. Everett, no doubt, judging by the silver Celtic knot necklace wrapped around the stems. Not her special necklace, the one her daddy give her, though. She'd part with that over her dead fuckin' body. Fearless; that was my son's Queen.

"I love you, brother. I'm gonna miss the hell out of you, but I guess I understand. I ain't mad. I can't be. That's not the way I want to leave things between you an' me."

I closed the lid softly and Dray stepped up next to me and helped me secure the hasps on the fancy-ass box's lid. I was grateful for it, seein' as my vision was too blurred to do it myself without his help. I swallowed hard. Put my cigarette out on the sole of my boot, and dropped it in a half-full glass of beer on one of the nearby tables.

I looked over Trig, Reave, Dray, Ghost, and Rev, all standing by, and said, "Let's do this, boys."

They helped me shoulder the burden of my friend in his casket and we carried our brother out the front door, the rest of the club standing around watching us, somber and hurting, ready as much as I was for it to be over. Marcie reached out and lightly grazed the back of my hand hanging at my side with her fingertips and I felt myself stand a little straighter.

We loaded Doc into the back of the hearse and got ready to take him on his final ride. I always fuckin' hated that it was in a cage, but they didn't make a bike for caskets.

The roar of the bikes was almost too much for my aching head, making my skull vibrate so hard I felt like my fuckin' face was gonna slide off. I shook my head as Marcie got on the back of my bike and resolutely told myself there was no fucking up today; I had precious cargo on board behind me. It was one thing if I biffed it on my own, but it wasn't gonna happen with her ridin' with me.

I led the pack, the officers riding as a vanguard in front of the hearse while the rest of the club and all of the out-of-towners followed up. I gave a nod to the police officers escorting us, and they ran interference, stopping traffic and the like. It was the one fuckin' time the law and my club was on the same team. Funerals. I started thinkin' that, maybe, with life calming down like it was, that I should ask Marcie what the club could do charity-wise to better cement with the good ol' boys in blue that we meant what we said: we were legit and tryin' to stay that way.

I let the thoughts go as we approached the cemetery. After all, Rome weren't built in a fuckin' day and today, of all days, was no day to start that shit.

We made it to the cemetery, my head throbbing in time to the chugging of my bike's engine as I backed it to the curb, first in line. The rest of my brothers pulled their bikes up, some across the road, so there was a narrow gauntlet of bikes behind the hearse. We got off our motorcycles, and the girls drifted up grave-side with some of the out-of-towners while the rest of us went to get Doc. Marcie kissed me quick, and gave me a reassuring squeeze of the hand before she joined Sunshine for the short trudge up the little hill to the man-made plateau our brothers rested on.

"Y'okay, Pops?" Dray asked as I looked up that hill to the gathering.

I sighed, "Yes, but no, Son."

He nodded, and Trigger rumbled, "I hear that."

"Let's bring him home, boys."

There were mumbles and grunts of assent and Trig opened up the back of the hearse, the driver from the funeral home standing by in case we needed any technical know-how. The shiny black box slid almost silent on the hearse's thingamajig, and we lifted the burden of our fallen man onto our shoulders, knowing the weight of his passing would sit on our hearts long after we put his physical body into the ground.

We marched up the hill, lined up to either side of the open grave, and lowered our man onto the canvas straps of the hoist that would take him down into the cold, dank earth. It was about this point, I was supposed to say some shit, but this time was... I don't know. It was hard. Not as hard as when it was Tilly going into the ground, but still difficult for me.

We stood around the grave a long time while everyone waited for me to speak.

"I don't think he'd want us to be sad, rather I think he'd expect us all to be... I don't know... relieved? Relieved to know he ain't hurtin' no more. Relieved to know he's with Chandra now, and glad he went out on his own fuckin' terms because, you know, fuck the man."

I raised a fist and pumped it twice into the air about shoulder height, halfheartedly. A few grunts of assent, and a couple of chuckles swept through the gathering.

"What I don't think he banked on was just how much we were going to miss his sorry ass. How much his wisdom meant to us, and how much he changed all of our lives for the better. Not just as a doctor, but as our brother, as our friend and confidante." I sucked in a breath and blew it out slow.

"Doc had a way about him. He kept our secrets, shared and soothed our pain both physical and emotional, and was always the one brother we could always count on to be there for us in our darkest fuckin' hours when it felt like no other brother understood."

More noises of agreement, soft weeping from the women.

"He stitched us up, he birthed our children, he made sure we were all right, no matter what. He took care of us, and life ain't gonna be the same without him. Not only did this club lose one of our best men, this town lost the best damned doctor that it's ever seen."

Cheers, some whistles and applause.

"So pour one out for Doc. After all he's fuckin' done for us, he's more 'n earned a fuckin' drink or two in the afterlife."

I gave a nod and they lowered my best friend's casket into the ground. I reached into the pocket of my jacket for the mini-bottle of Doc's favorite booze and cracked the seal. I poured it over the shiny black carapace of his casket and walked.

The women threw in white roses, the men poured their shots, and one by one we went back to the bikes. I sighed and murmured, "See you next week, you old bastard. You too, baby."

Marcie slipped her hand in mine and squeezed, I glanced over to her and she gave me a tight-lipped smile, the corners of her light blue eyes fanned with wrinkles with how tight they were, her pain, her empathy for what I was feeling in that moment palpable. I gave her a brave smile in return, but fuck if I was feeling anything like brave in that moment.

"Y'all have run of the house," I called out to the out-of-town club members, members from other chapters who'd come to pay their respects. I jammed my helmet back on my head and said, "I got business."

"Keep the dirty side down, brother," one of the Presidents from another chapter called out, and I gave a nod. I got onto my bike and Marcie got on behind me. Dray gave a nod and I pulled out, he followed, and we knew Ev would be right behind us with my grandson.

It probably wasn't the most ideal fuckin' day to have Sunday dinner with the two damn families, but there honestly wasn't any better day either. All I knew was I was ready for some fuckin' food.

28

M arcie…

I walked in my back door with Dragon on my heels and practically right into Bobby. The girls were at the table, setting it, while Rich and Jimmy were in the living room foolin' over some damn game on the TV.

"What're you doin' here?" I cried.

"Thought you always told me I was still part of the family," Bobby said, bending to kiss my cheek.

"Well, today wasn't exactly the day I wanted to do this, but Dragon, Bobby – Bobby, this here is Dragon and that's his son, Dray. Dray's lady, Everett, is on her way with their son, Stephen."

The TV had shut off and Rich and Jimmy had wandered up to stand in the archway from the kitchen to the living room while the girls stood in the archway from the kitchen to the dining room. The tension in the room was so thick you'd like to cut it with a knife.

"Where were you, Mamma?" Devon asked and Dylan tried to elbow her older sister into silence, scowling at her.

"Well, if you must know, I was at a funeral, girls," I said and I felt like an intervention was in the offing, but boy I tell you – not today, Satan. Not. To. Day.

Rich was the one to extend the olive branch. "Was real sorry to hear about your man, Dragon."

"Thank you, son," Dragon said. He swallowed hard. "Your boys on the motorcycle patrol did us proud on the funeral procession escort."

Rich and Jimmy both smiled and gave a nod at that.

"We'll miss Doc," Dray said. "He was the best of us."

Dragon nodded and reached blindly for his son's shoulder and gripped it, giving his son a bit of a shake back and forth.

"Knock, knock!" a voice called from outside, and I shooed people with my hands.

"Boys, to the living room, let Everett and the baby in. Shit, it's crowded in here. I don't think I thought this through." I worried and fussed over getting everyone settled and out of the way so I could cook. To my girls' credit, they may not have known where I was or what I was up to, but they had what I'd had in the fridge in the oven for me. Well, as much as would fit.

"Tried to get it going for you Mamma," Dylan murmured and I hugged her one-armed, proud of her, and kissed her temple.

"You girls do me proud," I said, but Devon was already aside with Everett and her little man, both of them just talkin' away. I felt a tight-ness, a worry, in my chest ease.

There wasn't much more awkwardness, until Bobby opened his fat head at the dinner table.

"So, uh, you don't mind me askin', what happened to your man?" My knife hit the plate with a clatter when it slipped from my nerveless fingers. I felt my face flame with embarrassment.

"Bobby Lanham!" I admonished. "That is not something to ask as polite dinner conversation."

Devon had the grace to look horrified at her father, too, saying, "I'm with Mamma on this one, Daddy. Je-sus!"

"What?"

"It's all right," Dragon's deep voice rumbled across the place settings and everyone quieted down.

Dray picked up and said, "Doc was sick, none of us knew. He died like we live, by his own choice, his own methods. We ain't gotta like it, but we *do* understand it."

"Oh, so it was suicide, then?" Bobby asked.

"Daddy!" Dylan cried and I put a hand to my forehead.

"What?" he asked and I didn't know what was worse, the fact the big dumb ox had asked in the first place, or that he was genuinely clueless as to why he shouldn't be askin' in the first place.

Bobby gave me a look from across the table and said, "Well, what d'you expect, Marcie? It's not like we know anything about 'em to know what t' ask."

Dragon's gaze roved over my face and he cocked his head slightly, "That's all right, I think that may be our fault to a certain extent." Dray even looked at his father like he'd growed a second head at that. Dragon smiled at me and said, "I told Marcie we were a private people, and she's the kind of woman to take things like that to heart. She probably didn't want to share anything out of turn."

"Oh, well, yeah… That's my Marcie," Bobby said.

"Maybe once, Bobby, but we're divorced, now," I reminded him gently, under my breath.

"Sorry." He colored slightly, "Just used to usin' the phrase," he said and sounded genuinely a bit guilty.

"Look, I'm fine, y'all. Dragon and his family are good people. We probably should have rescheduled this whole dinner thing for any other day, but he insisted we not cancel."

"We don't back out of our commitments," Dray said.

"No, no, you do not," I agreed.

Everett looked over to Dray, baby Stephen in her lap, and the look of love and adoration in her eyes, and the look Dray gave back; my girl Devon fell in love with them as a family right then and there, I think. It was cemented when Everett reached over under the table and she and Dray twined fingers beneath it.

"Aw," Devon said fondly, "How long have you two been together?"

"A few years," Everett said softly.

"Not long enough," Dray said, smiling. "Then again, 'forever' doesn't seem like it'd be long enough, either."

I glanced at Dragon who was smiling softly at me and I returned the smile. Thankfully, the subject shifted from sad to happier things after that and the awkwardness of the initial contact between our families was dispelled. Kind of hard to stay awkward when the whole table was melting into a puddle of goo at the romance between Everett and Dray. It was nice to know that Dragon's son, despite his dark and brooding looks, was a real chip off the old block. His daddy had a fine way with words too, enough to make my heart flutter every time he spoke.

It was a special family joining mine at the table. I was proud of my girls. My family? It was a special family, too.

I was at the sink, washing up after dessert and my girls' fabulous meal when Dragon came up behind me and put his hands on my hips he laid a reverent kiss on the side of my neck and murmured, "Dray says the natives are getting restless."

Dray had left right after dinner, kissing Everett and his son good-bye.

Everett had smiled up at her man like he hung the moon and stars, and he'd gone after some message had come through on his phone.

Didn't take long for Stephen to start to fuss and Everett sighed, "I should get going too, get him down for a nap. Ugh, his ma needs one, too." I chuckled and hugged her, kissing her cheek.

"That's motherhood for you," I said. She packed herself and her little one into her car and left, too. Not long after, I turned to discover Dragon buried in his phone, peering through his readers and fat-thumbing it, cursing, all over the screen trying to text. He did it, because most of the younger guys in the club preferred communicating that way, via text, but I happened to know he hated it.

"Problems?" I asked.

"Nothin' I can talk about. Club business."

I chuckled lightly and murmured, "Sounds like code for drama. Some-body get their feelings hurt?"

He grinned at me and said, "Can't tell you that, learn to live with it, Sugar. That's this life."

"Alright," I said, knowing damn well he'd fill me in when we weren't sittin' in the middle of a corn field. Rich and Jimmy were eying us from the living room and Devon and Dylan were staring at us, appre-hensive, from where they were gathering up plates and dishes from the dining room to bring to me.

I rolled my eyes and Dragon grinned, his eyes on me. He didn't even have to turn and look.

"It ain't nothin' illegal, boys and girls, it's just none of your business," he said kindly. I laughed a little at the looks on their faces and he gave me a quick kiss goodbye.

He said, "I better git before someone burns the club down by accident. Girls, thank you for a wonderful meal."

"You're welcome," Dylan said, while Devon stood next to her, mouth agape.

"See you later?" Dragon asked me.

"Probably *after* your house guests leave. I don't know about you, but I'm getting too old for nights like last night."

He chuckled and pulled on his fingerless riding gloves from his inside jacket pocket saying, "Truth be told, I'm right there with you. I need to leave the hard partying to the young bucks."

"Ride safe," I told him and he smiled and ducked his head in a nod as he pulled the door shut behind him. A moment later, his motorcycle fired up and he rode on down the gravel drive.

"Hard partying?" Bobby called from the living room. "I thought you was at a funeral."

"I was," I called back, rinsing the colander. "A biker's funeral."

"How are they different from any other person's funeral?" Devon asked and I could hear the genuine curiosity in her voice.

"Ever see an Irish wake on TV?"

"Can't say that I have," Jimmy said.

I smiled, "Well, let me tell you what I can, then…" and I did. Heavily editing out the drugs that some of the members were indulging in last night, the small orgy on the pool table, and the fist fight that damn near broke out – which it sounded like to me was in the thick of it, and caused Dray, then Dragon, to leave early. Of course, it weren't none of the local men, but some of the club members from out of town engaging in that fool behavior.

I tried to explain the whole 'club as a whole versus chapter' thing to the kids, but Jimmy, bless his heart, just wasn't catching on. My smart girl, Dylan, came to the rescue.

"It's like the government, Jimmy. We're the United States of America, but every state has their own rules. There's federal level, or the club as a whole, then there's state level, or your chapters."

"Oh, that makes sense," Jimmy nodded and I had to laugh and shake my head.

"I dunno if they'd take kindly to bein' compared to The Man, but it's as good a comparison as any," I said, handing a plate to Dylan to dry.

"You seem real happy, Mamma," she said, out of the blue, and I nodded.

"I am real happy," I said.

"Well, that's good," Bobby said with a big long stretch.

"Y' leavin'?" I asked.

"I am," he said.

"Take it Dragon passed whatever bullshit test you were runnin' him up against."

"Eh, he did, for now."

"Bobby Lanham!" I flicked my dishcloth at him and he put his hands up.

"Hey!"

"Hate to admit it," Rich said with a haggard sigh, "But when it comes to this town, we need 'em."

"What?" Devon demanded.

"It's true. Police force ain't what it should be for a town this size. *They* keep bigger criminal elements at bay around here, allowing us to focus our efforts. The rule of the street is very different from the law. It's kind of this fucked-up symbiotic relationship – but it's there."

"They're not bad people," I chimed in.

"I don't know that I'd go that far," Jimmy said dubiously, and I scowled at him.

"What? I've seen them case files, Mamma Marcie. It's rough stuff."

It was, as far as I was concerned, in the past, as well. Of course, there was no tellin' these pigheaded children that. I wiped off my hands on the dish towel over my shoulder and sighed.

"Look, y'all. I know you're worried, but I like Dragon. A lot. Hell, I would even go as far as to say I love that man, dearly. Now, he's not goin' away, and he's not as bad as all that. What's done is done, and there ain't no changin' it, and he knows that. But he's a changed man, lookin' for his salvation and I do believe that." I said the last giving Devon a sharp look as she opened her mouth to interrupt.

"Now, y'all are gonna have to get used to his bein' around, because he ain't goin' anywhere. Y'all are just gonna have to consider my house Switzerland from now on. Y'hear me?"

"I can live with that," Rich said with a shrug and everyone else turned to look at him, sorta horrified.

"Look, as bad as the Sacred Hearts' reputation is, I gotta give 'em something. They've always protected this town as much as they could from any blowback. I mean, look at that thing a couple a years ago with that club they disappeared. We was havin' all kinds of problems with robberies and burglaries happenin'. They started beefin' with the Sacred Hearts, the next thing you know, they been run outta town, and the crime rate all but evaporated."

"You sayin' the biker gang in our back yard makes less work for you, so you *like* them?"

Rich shrugged again and said, "If the shoe fits. I'll admit, I'm not keen on the Sacred Hearts bein' here, but at the same time, sometimes it is better the devil you know."

"What makes you say that?" I asked, and he wouldn't look at me.

Finally he said, "Anybody that can make a Mexican drug cartel not only cease operations but cease to exist – that ain't somebody I wanna be on their bad side, you know?"

"No, I don't know…" I trailed off.

"I ain't stickin' around for this, even though it does sound like a facinatin' bedtime story," Bobby said. He kissed my cheek and made for the back door.

"Well, all right, then. See you later," I called.

"Thanks for dinner," he said, shutting the back door and going down the back steps.

"Now, what're you gettin' on about over there."

Rich sighed. "The story goes, maybe nine or ten years back, the Sacred Hearts fucked up, or at least the cartel *thought* they fucked up, and so they gunned down their clubhouse. Dragon's wife, and several of the members at the time, didn't make it."

"The rest of the club, well, they had their funeral, then went to ground for a month or two, then shit got real, south of the border. There was some real rough stuff in the files, Mamma Marcie."

"Like what?" I asked, hollowly, the first creeping sensation of fear making itself known at the look on my son-in-law's face.

"Well, and I hate to tell you this, the first shot fired in retaliation was the bikers skinned a man alive and nailed his skin to one of the cartel leader's front doors. It only got *worse* from there."

I swallowed hard, my mouth suddenly dry, and had a hard time reconciling the horror story with the men and women I'd met. I didn't know what it said about me that my mind immediately justified the horrible action with *But they killed his wife…*

"I don't think I want to hear any more of this nonsense," I said, shaking my head.

"Mamma! It's not nonsense," Devon exclaimed. "These are dangerous people! We don't want nothin' to happen to you!"

"Oh! Ain't nothin' gonna happen to me, girls!" I sighed and realized there weren't no way I was gonna make them see what I did when it came to Dragon. That nothin' was gonna happen, because that man didn't make the same mistake twice.

There weren't nothin' gonna happen to me that God didn't intend, anyhow. Dragon had no control over my gettin' old, or drawing cancer or some other disease out of life's deck. That just was what it was. When it came to somethin' happening to me *because* of him, though. No. I didn't see it. It wasn't even on my radar as a possibility. Still, good luck tellin' my family that.

"I love you," I said to all of 'em in the ensuing silence. "Now I love him, too." I leaned back against the counter, all eyes on me and shook my head, disappointed in my girl Devon for the first time in I don't know how long... maybe ever. It wasn't the same kind of disappointment over a bad grade, or a bad hair color choice. This was a deeply-rooted disappointment and I had to pause and think on how to say it out loud.

Dylan looked at her sister the same way I was feelin' and as much as I hated to do it, I had to drop a hard truth on my very pregnant daughter about making snap judgments.

"I honestly thought I raised you better 'n this, Devon Lanham."

"Mamma, what're you talkin' about?" she demanded.

I sighed, "You're about to become a mamma yourself, so you'll know yourself in a few years' time, but right now? I am about as deeply disappointed in you as I have ever been."

Her mouth dropped open in shock and she looked at Dylan.

"Don't look at me for help," Dylan declared and crossed her arms. Devon's eyes glassed over and Rich got up and went over to his wife.

"Now, Mamma Marcie, I don't…"

"Shut it," I declared and whatever he'd been about to say, died.

"This is between me and my daughter, and I can't be sure you ain't the one who put these ideas toward hatin' that man in her head."

Devon looked confused, "I don't hate anybody!" she declared, horrified.

"Really?" I demanded. "You could have fooled me! Ever since he first set foot in this house, you've had your nose in the air actin' like he's the devil incarnate. Need I remind you, your Mamma's the one who killed *his* friend and *his* brother? Not the other way around."

She shut her mouth and even Rich had the grace to look embarrassed. I shook my head.

"He ain't done nothin' where I'm concerned except shown me forgiveness and grace and y'all been up in here scrutinizing and judgin' him at every turn, makin' every excuse as to why he is a bad man and somebody who can't change or be saved and I'm tired of it."

Silence stretched between me and my family and I honestly couldn't be more pained. I shook my head and said, "Y'all get out except Dylan. I don't want y' here right now."

"Mamma…" Devon looked a little lost and I shook my head.

"I mean it. Out. Right now. I can't even look at y'all."

"Mamma Marcie…" Rich tried and I raised my eyebrows. He shut up and nodded. "Next Sunday, then?" he asked.

I nodded, "As always."

I waited for them to collect their things and sighed when they pulled up the driveway. Dylan looked at me and made a somewhat cringy face and asked, "Get the bourbon out?"

"God, yes, child."

She laughed slightly and said, "I know Devon has always been the more uptight of the two of us, but Jesus Christ."

"I think it's just them hormones and her lookin' to be a new mother," I said, and dropped into a seat at the kitchen table.

Dylan trotted off to the liquor cabinet and brought back one of my bottles and I wrinkled my nose and shook my head. She looked a bit startled and said, "The *good* shit?"

I nodded, "The good shit."

"Wow, I thought it was bad but I didn't think it was *that* bad," she said, and came back with the correct bottle this time. She set it on the table and went to the cabinet above the sink and brought back two glasses.

She poured a splash in each and I raised my eyebrows. She blinked and added a little more to my glass. I nodded and leaned forward wearily and slid it towards me, taking a drink and relishing the smooth burn.

"She really hurt your feelings, huh?" my youngest asked me, and I nodded tiredly.

"I understand it," I said, "At the same time I don't, you know?"

"She's just worried, Mamma, she's goin' to have her first child and she's scared and probably feels like her body's in control and not her, and so she's tryin' to control everything else." Dylan shrugged and sipped her bourbon, putting down her glass and smiling at me.

I groaned and put a hand to my face, I didn't even think about that. I probably should have. I mean, she was overdue and ready to go any minute and as big as a house. I sighed and said, "You're too smart for your own good and I am the worst mother ever."

She laughed, "No, you're not! Everything you said was absolutely right. She's not being fair – and I'm not either. I'm just better at keepin' quiet about it."

I started at my younger daughter, who shrugged simply and rolled her lips. I shook my head. *Worst mother ever or best one? Sometimes it's hard to decide.*

"I love you girls, with all my heart," I said finally. "You're the best things I ever did with my life."

"Thanks, Mamma... We love you too, more than anything, we just want you to be okay. Could you imagine if it was one of us with one of them before you learned all you did? A year ago? Two years ago?"

I thought about it and said, "I'd kill yah."

"Exactly."

I sighed and said, "Here's to my rebellious teenage years – in my fifties."

Dylan clicked glasses with me and wincing, said, "Mamma, I think they call that a mid-life crisis."

29

D**ragon...**
"Then what'd she say?" I asked.

"That little shit," Marcie said savagely. "She says to me, 'Mamma, I think that's what they call a mid-life crisis.' Can you believe that shit?"

I laughed outright and couldn't stop laughing right away if I'd wanted to. I wiped tears out of the corner of my eye and said, "I can see right where she gets it from."

"Oh, you!" Marcie's smile came right on through the line and it was like sunshine against my ear.

"I miss you," I told her suddenly, out of the blue.

"I miss you, too," she said. "How long until I get to see you again?"

I sighed and said, "Soon as I sort this shit out."

"I still can't believe you're in *Detroit.*"

"Duty calls," I said ruefully.

"Well, you'll have to tell me all about it when you get home."

"It's a promise," I told her.

"All right."

"Okay, love you." I cleared my throat. "Bye for now."

"Love you, too, honey. Bye-bye."

I smiled and hung up the phone, sticking it into the inside pocket of my jacket along with my glasses. Nox looked over from where he was leaning against his bike scowling, and asked, "Can we get the fuck out of here?"

"Soon as we find this little rat-bastard," I said flicking my cigarette into the gutter.

"I was likin' my nice, quiet life," my brother muttered and I raised my eyebrows.

"That makes two of us, but you know how it goes."

He nodded.

It had gone a little beyond a fist fight at the club; one of the Detroit chapter brought a knife into it, cut one of the Denver boys real bad, then took his punk ass off. Detroit, to their credit, were just about as pissed off with his pussy actions as us, so here we all were, tryin' to find the little bastard and take back what was ours. He didn't deserve to wear our colors. By unanimous vote, his chapter had put his ass out bad for runnin', so the chase was on until we got his fuckin' cut back and made sure his ink was blacked.

"Yeah, thanks." Data got off his phone and raised his eyebrows.

"Fucked-up, burned-out neighborhood east of I-75." Data said.

"That's a fairly decent sized area," Rebel, one of the local boys, declared.

"Uh-huh," Data said, only half-listening. He was scribbling on a notepad and when he finished, he ripped the page off the spiral wire and slapped the piece of paper against Rebel's chest.

"Red house, boarded-up windows, mid-block," he said and I chuckled.

Rebel shook his head and said, "Don't know how the hell you get this stuff," he said.

"Above yer paygrade," I said, chuckling, and put my helmet on my head. Reaver mounted up next to me eagerly. In case anyone had any doubt that I weren't playin', I had invited him along.

"Well, all right then. Let's get it done," Tank declared, and I gave a nod.

Didn't take us long to find the house, took us a little longer to find the squirrely little bastard. We did what needed doing, and then, rather than stick around, we started straight for home. The parts of the ride where my mind wasn't a quiet blank, it was stuck on how much I was glad we were movin' away from doing shit like that. It also kept wrapping around the fact, that unintentional as it may have been, I'd brought a lot of drama into Marcie's life.

I was wrestling with that by quite a bit, and by the time we pulled into the club a day or two later, all I wanted was a shower, about twelve hours' worth of sleep, and to just get the bad news over. I'd come to the conclusion that when it came to Marcie, I just loved her too damn much to make her life hell.

I laid down to sleep and passed right the fuck out, and I think I dreamed…

"You are one dumb fuckin' son of a bitch, you know that?"

I opened my eyes to Doc sitting in the recliner in the corner of my room and scowled.

"Am I dreaming?" I asked, out loud, my voice rusty from smoking and the road.

"Well you damn sure ain't awake, or did you forget I offed myself?"

I rolled my eyes and asked, "So why're you here?"

"Hopefully to knock some damn sense into that fat head of yers. That woman is a good woman, and tough as all get out. Now I know it ain't the same, but it's good, and contrary to your stupid belief that you don't deserve nothin' good, you do. So suck it the fuck up and keep on keepin' on, brother."

"This your idea of a pep talk? 'Cause if it is, you suck at it."

He laughed, blue eyes twinkling, and nodded, "That was always your thing, the pep talks. I'm just here trying to prevent you from making the second-worst mistake of your life."

He knew I would never let losing Tilly go as my number one, so I nodded and asked, "How's life in the afterlife?"

My best friend grinned at me and he shook his head, "You'll see when you get here, which ain't gonna be for some time yet. Just don't do anything stupid in the meantime." He got up, I blinked, and he was gone. Just like that. I let my head fall back onto the pillow and closed my eyes again, or at least I think I did. Really wasn't accountin' for the fact I never even really woke up in the first place.

In any case, when I woke up for what I think was for real, I opened my eyes to a pair of true blue ones under a vibrant copper shock of hair. Marcie smiled at me and stretched luxuriously and I couldn't help but smile, too.

"What're you doing here?" I murmured, and cupped her cheek, and damn if Doc wasn't right. I could no more crush her heart than I could my own, by walkin' away from her. Still, I felt a kind of stiff sadness in my chest over it. The feeling like I was dooming her to somethin' by havin' her by my side.

Didn't seem like she much had the same opinion, though, so I had to stuff it down for now and chalk it up to just my usual brooding.

"I called, your boy answered your phone said you left it on the bar. Said you was back."

She was smiling and way too excited for just me bein' back here so I asked, "What ain't you tellin' me?"

"It's a girl!" she crowed, throwing her arms around my neck and it took me a minute to think what she was talkin' about.

"Devon?" I asked.

"Uh-huh!"

"Well, I'll be damned!" I grinned, sharing in her joy, then it hit me and I pulled back to look her in the eyes.

"You left the hospital, your daughter, your new grandbaby, just to see me?"

"Well, yeah. I missed you, and mamma and the baby could use the rest... I wanted to see you, to tell you."

I silenced her by covering her mouth with mine and I couldn't tear her clothes off fast enough. I lucked out that she was wearin' one of her long skirts, so really, all I had to get through were her panties.

They gave with a swift jerk, the material making a popping noise before tearing away. Marcie cried out, but her hips rose and she helped me get between her thighs, her mouth finding mine and feeding at it, but I was the one taking all the nourishment her kiss could provide. I shoved my cock against her and pretty much dry-humped her like an awkward teenager for a few, both to make sure she was excited enough to take me and because it felt so damn good.

Sliding into her was like coming home, and the satisfied moan she let off into my mouth tasted like love and hope and a brighter future. I was surprised to realize I wanted it. I was done punishing myself, isolating myself, and the way Doc died? Alone... I didn't want that to be me. I was probably going to hell anyway, and I loathed that I may or may not be dragging Marcie down there with me. Yet, as I pushed myself into her, her hips rose to meet mine, and it was pretty clear to me she was willing and along for the ride.

The way her hands cupped my face, the fierce look in those blue eyes as I struck a swift but easy rhythm. The way the bottom of her foot caressed up and down my calf… she was fully present when we had sex and I loved that about her. That she was *here* and *present* all of the time when she was with me, a soul-deep connection despite my malfunction.

I let myself drown in her soft skin, her wet heat, her delicate scent, and I didn't want to come up for air. It was startling, frightening, to care about her as much as I did. I'd never in a million years thought there would be a second chance for a bastard like me.

"What're you lookin' at me like that for?" she whispered, her fingertips gently grazing my cheek.

"Just so in love with you it hurts," I murmured back, and the smile that she graced me with was enough to turn my world on its end, which ironically, was the direction it needed to go for everything to just fall into place.

EPILOGUE

ELEVEN YEARS LATER…

M arcie…

"He's struggling," I murmured into the phone, my heart breaking, my voice wavering with barely-suppressed tears.

"Is it time? Should I get over there?"

I nodded, realized Dray couldn't see it, and said, "That would be best, yeah."

He hung up without saying another word and I lowered my phone to the kitchen counter. Dragon let out another rumbling cough from his hospice bed in our living room and those tears I'd been holding back slipped free.

I went over to where the machine was set up and checked his oxygen levels; they were bad. Real bad. He looked at me from over the cannula in his nose supplying his cancer-ravaged lungs with oxygen, his face sunken, his color sallow and he reached out a hand, weakly.

"Gonna… gonna miss you, babe," he rasped out, and I took his hand and squeezed my eyes shut, sobbing quietly. He chuckled in that way of his, which ended with another fit of coughing, which led to gasping and an almost ten-minute struggle to get his air back.

"Come up here, read to me like you do," he rasped. I nodded and lowered the bed rail on one side and climbed up into bed with him. I had just lifted the book we were reading from the rolling tray table when Dray came in the back door.

"How you doin', Pops?" he asked with false brightness.

"I'm dyin', son. How you think I'm doin'?" he asked. "Sit down and listen a while with me. Marcie –" He gasped for breath. "Marcie's gonna read to me."

Dray pulled up a chair and reached through the railing, grasping his father's hand and sitting with us while I read.

Midway through, Dragon raised a hand and said weakly, "I love you, all of you. My boy, his wife, my girl, her girls, my grandson, the club… I love all of you."

"We love you, too, Pops," Dray said. "Try and get some rest."

I closed the book and carefully cuddled into Dragon's side as he drifted. It was the last thing he said to us before slipping into what can only be described as a sort of death-coma, that transitional place where all you could do was pump him morphine and hope he wasn't in any pain.

I looked across at Dray and the sorrow in his eyes made my heart bleed.

"It's gonna be okay, Mamma," he said. "He'll be with us forever."

It was a cold comfort to my ravaged heart, even though I knew it was true. He would be with us forever. Forever and beyond. He was Dragon, and that was how he was.

Tenacious, fearless, and the only rules he followed between heaven and earth were his own.

AUTHOR'S NOTE

Dear readers, thank you for holding on with me through the four year journey that has been The Sacred Hearts MC. It breaks my heart that their story is concluded, but at the same time, it is time. I hope you'll stick with me to see where the Indigo Knights go as I have a lot planned for them. Much love, and all the best from me to you.

ALSO BY A.J. DOWNEY

Indigo Knights

1. Her Thin Blue Lifeline
2. His Cold Blue Command
3. A Low Blue Flame
4. His Wild Blue Rose
5. Her Pained Blue Silence
6. A Cold Blue Call
7. Her Reluctant Blue Cavalier
8. Forged Under Fire
9. Under A Blue Moon
10. Sound of Blue Thunder

Sacred Hearts MC Pacific Northwest

1. Over the High Side
2. Wind Therapy
3. Apex of the Curve
4. Low Sided
5. Eating Asphalt
6. Hammer Down
7. Only Fool Riding

The Voodoo Bastards MC

1. Bourbon & Blood
2. Whiskey Shivers
3. Moonshine Lullabies
4. Cognac Secrets
5. Tequila Damnation

Iron Wraiths MC

1. Original Syn

2. Love & Fear

3. The Hangman's Rope

Royal Bastard MC: St. Augustine Chapter

1. Iron Hearts

Paranormal Romance (with Ryan Kells)

1. I Am The Alpha

2. Omega's Run

3. Hunter's End

Indigo City Darker (with Jared KingPacal Lain)

1. Triple Threat

2. Double Shot

Standalones

Synchronicity

ABOUT A.J. DOWNEY

A.J. Downey is a Pacific Northwest girl living in an East Tennessee world who finds inspiration from her surroundings, through the people she meets, and likely as a byproduct of way too much caffeine. She specializes in real and relatable romance stories featuring that real-life kind of love that everyone craves.

Stalker Information:

Website
www.ajdowney.com